## The ornate box began to glow. It rose from the coffee table and hovered in the air.

Sabrina reached for the box, but Harvey got to it first. His fingers pressed against something warm and he jerked, startled.

The box flew open in all directions. An eerie, blue light swirled out of it, accompanied by a strange, bell-like clanging. The blue light became a wind that whirled around the room, catching up small objects—including the group's project notebook.

Then, as the group looked on in amazement, the notebook landed on top of the flattend box. Valerie shouted, "I'll get it!"

She leaped forward to get the notebook, lost her balance, and flattened her hands on top of it. And she disappeared!

"Valarie!" Harvey shouted, reaching forward. And *he* disappeared!

"What's going on?" Libby cried. And she disappeared!

Then Sabrina was swept forward toward the box as if by unseen hands. And, like her friends, she vanished from sight.

## Sabrina, the Teenage Witch® books

Available from ARCHWAY Paperbacks

# Sabrina
## The Teenage Witch®

### Up, Up, and Away

**Nancy Holder**

**Based on Characters Appearing in Archie Comics**

**And based upon the television series
Sabrina, The Teenage Witch
Created for television by Nell Scovell
Developed for television by Jonathan Schmock**

**AN ARCHWAY PAPERBACK**
Published by POCKET BOOKS
New York  London  Toronto  Sydney  Tokyo  Singapore

AN ARCHWAY PAPERBACK *Original*

An Archway Paperback published by
POCKET BOOKS, a division of Simon & Schuster Inc.
1230 Avenue of the Americas, New York, NY 10020

ISBN: 0-671-02805-7

First Archway Paperback printing December 1999

10  9  8  7  6  5  4  3  2  1

Printed in the U.S.A.

IL: 4+

*For Belle Claire Christine Holder*
*and*
*Rebecca Morhaim*

A big *merci beaucoup* to Ingrid van der Leeden,
Rodger Weinfeld, Paul Ruditis, Howard Morhaim,
and Lindsay Sagnette.

# Up, Up, and Away

☆

# Chapter 1

☆

**A**nd in conclusion, that's how humankind learned how to fly," Sabrina Spellman said, tacking her group's somewhat wrinkled poster to the easel in front of the chalkboard. It hung there for about a second. Then the pushpin popped out and the poster divebombed to the floor.

*It figures,* she thought. *Everything else has gone wrong.* Their videotape was missing the sound . . . Valerie had accidentally dropped their project notebook in last night's spaghetti sauce . . . Sabrina had misnumbered her note cards and given her speech out of sequence.

And the poster had started to fly away on a strong breeze at school this morning, until Sabrina pointed it back when no one else was looking.

Her blond hair framed her red face as she flushed at the laughter of her Westbridge High classmates. Then,

1

bending down to pick up the poster, she heard a *rrrip*. Her brand-new black pants had just come apart at the seams.

*Just like this project,* she thought miserably. *And I was team leader.*

She tacked the large piece of posterboard back up, but it detached again and sailed toward the floor. This time she caught it, and the class broke into mocking applause.

The large red rectangle was labeled: "The History of Flight: From the Dream to the Reality." Beneath that were the words: "The Montgolfier Brothers: French Pioneers." It featured a drawing of two men dressed like George Washington, sitting on ornate wooden chairs tied with several colorful silk balloons. The chairs were rising into the clouds, to the delight of a quartet of onlookers in colonial-style costumes, one of whom just happened to be a blond girl holding a black cat.

Said black cat just happened to resemble Salem Saberhagen, the former warlock who lived in Westbridge with Sabrina and her two witchy aunts, Hilda and Zelda Spellman. He had been turned into a cat by the Witches' Council for trying to take over the Mortal Realm. Sabrina had drawn him in as a little in-joke.

But the reaction of her classmates to her presentation was anything but a joke. As she picked up her misnumbered note cards and returned to her seat, she thought, *Yikes. Tough crowd.*

Her boyfriend, Harvey Kinkle, nodded to her as she sat down. A member of her team, Harvey was a likable, friendly kind of guy, and good-looking, too. He gave her a crooked smile, his hazel eyes making half-moons in his face as he leaned toward her and said, "Great conclusion."

"But not-so-great speech," Sabrina muttered.

"No, it was good," her best friend, Valerie, assured her. "However, I think we're doomed. We didn't really have enough facts about the history of flight, even if you'd presented them in the correct order. I liked how you tried to distract them, though." The third member of the group, she sat in the chair behind Sabrina and rested her chin in her palms, her dark brown hair cupping her face.

"Oh, please." Seated to the left of Sabrina, Libby Chessler rolled her eyes. She was one of the most popular people at Westbridge High, and she had not been happy about being assigned to Sabrina's team . . . except for the fact that Harvey was on it. Over the years, she had made it more than clear that she wanted Harvey for herself. She couldn't figure out why he seemed to prefer "the freak," as Libby called Sabrina. Sabrina didn't know either, but she was glad he did.

"Well." Vice-principal Willard Kraft got up from the teacher's desk and walked in front of the blackboard. He was filling in for Sabrina's science teacher, and he was not a happy man.

"That had to be the worst project we've slogged through today," he grumbled. He pointed at the poster the team had made. "This presentation was neither a dream nor based in reality," he said, tapping the words on the poster. "It was a nightmare." He frowned at Sabrina. "To put it nicely."

"Wow, harsh," Sabrina murmured. "I'm not sure I like you nice."

"Excuse me, Miss Spellman? Do you have something to share with the class?" Mr. Kraft asked, peering over his glasses.

"I think we've shared enough for one day," Sabrina answered, squirming.

"I have some cookies in my locker," Valerie piped up, half-raising her hand. Her dark eyes were wide as she peered up at Mr. Kraft. "If you think sharing those will help any."

Mr. Kraft frowned at Valerie. "Are you trying to bribe me, Miss Burkhead?"

"No. No," she protested. Then she shrugged. "Unless it's going to work."

"What kind are they?" Mr. Kraft asked, then shook his head quickly. "I mean, of course I can't be bribed. This is a horrible project. Half the words in your notebook are incorrectly spelled," he continued, paging through their report. "And the other half are covered with spaghetti sauce. Miss Burkhead, aren't you the editor of the school paper?"

"Guilty, sir," she said. She sighed heavily. "I must have forgotten to spell-check it." She glanced at her friend and fearful leader. "I'm sorry, Sabrina."

"I could forgive that. With a D," Mr. Kraft said. "Because on balance, these diagrams of airplanes are actually pretty well done."

"Gee, thanks," Harvey said, brightening. "I did that on my Mac."

"But your actual facts are so wrong, I can do nothing

but flunk you." Mr. Kraft tapped his forehead and chuckled in astonishment. "Where on earth did you people get the idea that the Montgolfier brothers rose up into the sky on living room chairs?"

*"What?"* Sabrina leaned forward and eyed Libby. "That was the section *you* researched."

Libby flushed beet red and looked very guilty. "I . . . I must have gotten confused." She waved her hands in the air and batted her eyelashes at Mr. Kraft like a helpless damsel in distress. As head cheerleader, she often managed to persuade him to give her special privileges. Sabrina already knew what was coming, and she was not disappointed.

*Just really ticked.*

"Mr. Kraft, I don't think it's fair to include me in this . . . this farce of a project," Libby protested. "To be honest, I had very little to do with it."

"You can say that again," Sabrina grumbled. Libby had missed almost every single meeting of their group. During the work sessions she had managed to attend, she mostly did her nails and paged through fashion magazines.

Ignoring Sabrina, Libby folded her arms across her chest. "The entire project was badly organized. I wasn't sure what I was supposed to be doing from one minute to the next."

"That's because you weren't there from one minute to the next!" Sabrina cried.

*"I* had cheerleading practice." Libby sat up very straight and proud. "And other commitments having to do with school spirit."

"Well, Harvey managed to show up, and he had football practice," Sabrina shot back.

"And I had to spend hours editing the school paper," Valerie added. "But I still went. And I brought cookies." She glanced at Mr. Kraft. "White chocolate macadamia nut."

"Oh—my favorite," Mr. Kraft noted eagerly.

"The extras are what's in my locker," Valerie added.

"Well, I never eat cookies. I have to watch my figure," Libby cut in. "Because I care so much about this school."

"Well, if you'd cared half as much about this project, we wouldn't be in this mess," Sabrina said.

"Excuse me." Mr. Kraft raised his hands. "This is not the time or place for your bickering. Sabrina, as the team leader, it was your responsibility to schedule your meetings around the activities of your group members." He gestured to Libby. "We all know the heavy burden Libby carries as a cheerleader. Allowances must be made."

He put the project notebook on his desk. "Libby's going to pass. The other three are all getting F's."

"Hey, that's not fair!" Sabrina protested.

Mr. Kraft shrugged. "I'm a vice-principal. I don't have to be fair."

Harvey raised his hand. "Mr. Kraft, can't you give us another chance? We'll try harder. We promise."

Most people liked Harvey very much. Sometimes his laid-back attitude got him into trouble—it was a bit difficult for him to resist peer pressure—but more often, it smoothed over a difficult situation. That was one of the many things Sabrina appreciated about him.

"Not in a million years," the vice-principal said firmly.

"If I get an F, my parents won't let me have my party," Harvey said. He had been planning the get-together for three weeks, and he had told Sabrina he might be able to have a live band.

*If I get an F, I won't be able to go anyway,* Sabrina thought dismally. Her grades were down, way down. She had to pull them up or her aunts were going to ground her for a *month.*

"Please—give them another chance?" Libby smiled hopefully at Mr. Kraft.

*That request is not being made out of the goodness of her heart,* Sabrina thought. *She's already bought a hot new outfit to wear to Harvey's party.*

*She spent half of gym class telling me about it.*

"Well . . ." The vice-principal shrugged and smiled back at her. "Perhaps a second chance, then. All right." He pointed his finger at the four of them. "I want you to do some decent research. At least get the part about the Montgolfiers correct. And if you don't get it right this time . . ." He shrugged. ". . . Only Miss Chessler will receive a passing grade, in recognition of all she does for the school."

Sabrina huffed. Then the bell rang, ending all discussion.

She turned to the others. "Let's get together after last period," she said. "My house. We'll plan our battle strategy."

"I'm busy," Libby informed her, smoothing her curly dark hair away from her forehead. "I have an appointment with my mother's seamstress. My new cheerleading outfits need some alterations."

"Then we'll meet after your appointment. Say, five?" Sabrina asked wearily.

"I'll be there," Harvey informed her.

"I'll be there, too," Libby said quickly, glancing possessively at Harvey.

Valerie raised her hand. "Me, too." She rolled her large brown eyes. "Since the only thing I have to do tonight is approve all the copy for next week's edition of the paper."

"Let's just hope there are no words over two syllables in it," Libby said archly.

"And I have to read *A Tale of Two Cities*," Valerie added, as if she had nearly forgotten.

"The entire book?" Sabrina asked.

Valerie looked worried. "Why? Is it long?"

"It's just about the entire French Revolution," Libby said imperiously. *"I* already read it."

Valerie bit her lower lip. "Did it take forever?"

*"Oui."* Libby smiled sourly at her. "You'll never finish it in one night."

"Then how am I going to pass the test tomorrow?" Valerie wailed.

"That's an excellent question." Libby preened. "One that I don't have to answer, fortunately."

Sabrina looked at Valerie. "Why don't you go home and start reading *A Tale of Two Cities?* Then you'll be a little bit ahead by the time you get to my house."

"Ahead of what? The French Revolution?" Valerie asked. She looked panic-stricken. "Back then, if you didn't do what they wanted, they cut off your head!"

"What an enlightened age," Libby drawled. "Here, all you get is detention." She grinned at Valerie. "Or an F."

"So," Harvey said again, "Five." He smiled at Sabrina.

"You got it." She smiled back and headed for her locker. But as she dialed the combination, she thought, *How are we supposed to do any better on our project? We still can't work together.*

Then she thought, *I'll go home and ask my aunts. They'll know. They've been doing things together for hundreds of years.*

In the living room of the large Victorian where the Spellman witches made their home, Hilda Spellman glared at Zelda Spellman and said, "If you don't go away and leave me alone, I'll turn you into a newt."

"Just try it," Zelda flung back at her. "I'll turn you into a . . . an iguana!"

"Hi," Sabrina said with mock cheerfulness to her two aunts as she came through the front door. She was soaking wet from head to toe. "It appears you two caused a pretty awesome thunderstorm with your quarrel. It's *so* nice to see you getting along, as you have been doing for centuries upon centuries."

"Oh, Sabrina, we're sorry," Sabrina's Aunt Hilda said.

"Yes, dear. Let me zap you dry." Aunt Zelda pointed, and instantly Sabrina was raindrop-free.

Hilda, the younger of the Spellman witch sisters, wore her honey-colored hair short, and she often wore bows or headbands. She was a colorful dresser; she was also the shorter of the two, with a chipmunk smile and a gift for mischievousness that matched Sabrina's yen for adventure. She also played a mean violin.

Zelda, the intellectual, wore her blond hair slightly longer and tended to be more conservative in her attire. She was a physicist who had made important discoveries in both the Mortal Realm and the Other Realm. She was much more serious than Hilda, but she could cut loose and have a good time, too.

Both aunts understood that they had assumed an awesome responsibility when they had invited Sabrina to live with them. Sabrina had not even realized she was a half-witch with magic powers until her sixteenth birthday, when she'd levitated above her bed for the first time. Before they revealed the truth to her, she had assumed her aunts had invited her to stay with them because her divorced parents each had far-flung interests. Her mother, a mortal, was an archeologist on a dig in Peru; her father was in the "foreign service."

Little had she realized just how "foreign" that service was—Edward Spellman, her father, was a warlock who spent a great deal of his time inside a magic book. Luckily, she owned that book, and so she could consult with him from time to time when she was in a bind.

*Now might be a good time,* she thought. *Since these two are quarreling like—well, sisters.*

"What seems to be the problem?" Sabrina asked her aunts.

Zelda rolled her eyes. "The usual."

"I'll go with that," Hilda concurred. "It's the same thing we always fight about."

Sabrina managed to hide her chuckle. "Oh. And since that could be oh, about fifty different things, I'll just say, 'I hope you two work it out.' "

She went upstairs into her room and dumped her schoolbooks and sweater on the bed.

"Hey, watch it!" Salem the cat groused.

"Oops." Sabrina quickly grabbed up her books. She scanned the bed for the talking American shorthair who made his home with the three witches. "Did I smush you?"

"No, but I was planning to doze there next," Salem said. "Your books will be in the way."

The black cat was curled up on the seat of Sabrina's bay window.

"Oh, well, I beg your pardon," Sabrina said somewhat sarcastically. "I wouldn't want to clutter up your reserved napping sites in *my* room with *my* belongings." She dropped her books back on the bed.

"Plus, I left a hairball there," Salem added, burping.

"Oh, gross!" Sabrina cried. *"Salem!"*

"I tried to warn you." He licked his paw. "But does anyone ever listen to me?" He melodramatically flopped over on his side. "Not anymore. Once millions held their breath, waiting to hear what brilliant thing I would say next."

*"Millions?"* Sabrina drawled. As a warlock, Salem had attempted to take over the Mortal Realm. However, he had not succeeded, and the Witches' Council had punished him by turning him into a cat. The Spellman sisters were in charge of him, which was why he shared their house.

11

"Okay. Thousands. Or maybe hundreds. It's been so long," Salem retorted.

*However, even if it was only a dozen, he did have followers,* she reminded herself. *Which means that maybe he does know a thing or two about leadership. . . .*

"So, how did you get all those people to listen to you?" she asked.

"I promised them whatever they wanted." He yawned and stretched. "And speaking of listening, all this chitchat has worn me out. I usually sleep through rainy days."

He shut his eyes and started snoring.

Sabrina considered. What did each of her group members want? *Harvey wants to have his party. Libby wants Harvey. Valerie wants to get through* A Tale of Two Cities. *And I want a decent grade so I can go to Harvey's party.*

"Salem," she said, turning to the cat. He snored louder. *He's no help.*

She started to page through her magic book. Her father wasn't in, and she had no idea what kind of spell to perform to make the project go more smoothly. Or even if she could use magic in a case like this. She wasn't allowed to conjure up good grades, money, or any of a number of things that would make life in the Mortal Realm a lot easier. Playing fair where mortals were involved was a lesson she had had to learn the hard way . . . more than once.

With a sigh, she shut the book and changed into fresh gray pants and a gray boat-neck sweater. Then she decided to go downstairs to straighten up before the group showed.

*That includes making certain there are no stray magic spells around, too.*

She left her room and retrieved the magic feather duster from the linen closet. The closet was also the family's portal to the Other Realm. As she went downstairs, she waved the duster in the air. If there were any "magic bunnies" to sweep away, it would do the trick.

She caught one—the merest trace of a wish upon a star—and swept it up into the duster, where it disappeared.

To her surprise, her aunts were seated side-by-side on the sofa in the parlor, reading the current issue of *Witch-mopolitan* together.

"Wow, last time I saw you two we were about to open a reptile farm," she said.

"Oh, Sabrina, you know how it is with sisters," Aunt Zelda replied. "Well, actually, you don't. But trust me, you can bicker and fight for hundreds of years, and then it's all forgotten in an instant."

"I'm impressed," Sabrina said sincerely.

Hilda looked pleased. "Then our work here is done." She snapped the magazine shut.

"Hey, I wasn't finished with that page!" Zelda protested.

Hilda gave her sister a knowing look. "You weren't reading the article, Zelly. Because it was all about what perfume you should wear, and you have no patience for that sort of thing. You were ogling that warlock in the tux."

Zelda shrugged. "A girl can dream."

"And a girl can ask her aunts for some help," Sabrina put in.

Hilda raised her brows expectantly. "That's what we're here for, Sabrina."

"That, and to teach you to use your powers responsibly . . . and make sure you grow into a mature young witch," Zelda added.

"I think you forgot to mention the part about me eating all my vegetables," Sabrina drawled.

"I was getting to that," Zelda assured her. "Now." She folded her hands. "What can we help you with?"

Sabrina thought for a moment. "Is it cheating to put a spell on the members of my science project group to make them get along better?"

"Yes," her aunts said at once.

With a groan, Sabrina flopped into the chair beside the couch. "Then you may as well ground me now. I'm going to flunk science."

"What's wrong, dear?" Zelda asked, very concerned.

"We had to do a report on the history of flight, and we did a terrible job, to be honest. For starters, we got some of our facts wrong. Like about the Montgolfier brothers."

Zelda brightened. "I have just the thing for you."

Sabrina clapped her hands. "You do?"

"Yes." Zelda's eyes shone. "Down in the basement."

Sabrina got to her feet. "What is it? A spell for—"

"At least a dozen books on the history of flight. Including some original sketches by Leo da Vinci. We dated a little," she added, looking dreamy-eyed. "I've always been partial to Italians."

"Books." Sabrina frowned. "Books, our group had. Lots of them. We just didn't use them very well."

Zelda gestured encouragingly at her. "Just go down there and see what I've got packed away. Maybe you'll find something to inspire you."

Groaning, Sabrina headed toward the basement. "Just once I'd like to wiggle my nose like those witches on TV and have everything go poof! and be solved in twenty-two minutes. But that doesn't happen in the real world."

She pointed open the basement door and started down the stairs.

"In the real world," she continued, muttering to herself, "you stand halfway down the basement stairs and gape in amazement at all the stuff your aunts have managed to collect in several centuries of living."

The basement was piled high with crates, barrels, and boxes. There was a unicycle and a complete miniature re-creation of Salem, Massachusetts—the town, not the cat . . . bolts of glittering fabric . . . a stuffed rhinoceros. A dungeon.

She didn't see any books. So she pointed her finger and said a spell.

*"Before I search through every object,*
*Help me with my science project!"*

Immediately a strange-looking box appeared on the step below the one she was standing on. It was made of dark wood and inlaid with shiny metallic moons, stars, and sparkly comets.

She picked the box up. It was heavy for its size.

"Did you find what you're looking for, dear?" Zelda called.

"I'm not sure," Sabrina called back. It began to hum and glow. The stars and moons started spinning, and one of the comets shot across the room.

"But I think I'm about to find out," she added.

*Woo hoo!*

# Chapter 2

☆

☆

As Sabrina carried the dark wooden box upstairs, she watched it glisten and gleam with a magical kaleidoscope of colors. The comets and stars pulsated in perfect rhythm with the rumble of the late-afternoon New England thunderstorm.

"Hey," she said excitedly, "look at this."

But there was no one in the living room. Her aunts had gone somewhere else.

Lightning crackled and the rain poured down outside as Sabrina sat down on the sofa and examined the box. Turning it over in her hands, she experimentally tapped one of the stars.

Immediately, the box flashed with a brilliant rainbow glow. The section of the box with the star emblazoned on it slid out. It was a little drawer.

"What's this?" Sabrina asked. Inside the drawer was a note written on silver paper with glittery letters. She took the note out and read, *"As the rain falls from the cloud."*

"As the rain fall from the cloud, what?" she said. "What is this thing?"

She tapped another star. Again the box flashed with multicolored brilliance, and another little drawer popped open. As with the first drawer, there was a note inside, also silvery, also glittery.

*"Before the ceasing of the rain,"* she read. "Now, what's that supposed to mean?"

"Try chanting 'Queen to Queen's level three,' " said a voice just above Sabrina's right shoulder. She looked up to see the big black cat perched on the back of the sofa.

"Salem," Sabrina said.

"In the fur." He bobbed his head. "Go on, say it. 'Queen to Queen's level three.' "

She frowned. "Why? What's it mean?"

Salem raised his front paw and licked it nonchalantly. "I have absolutely no idea. But they're always saying it on the old *Star Trek* series, and it sounds very cool. Don't you think?"

"You watch way too much TV," Sabrina scolded him.

"It passes the time." He sighed. "There's not a lot to do when you're a cat. Life was a lot more fun when I was taking over the world."

Sabrina wagged a finger at him. "You know, if you showed a little remorse the Witches' Council might reduce your sentence."

Salem sighed again. His tail flopped lazily across the

top of the sofa. "Oh, I've tried that. I sobbed until my fur fell out in huge clumps and not one of them bought my act. Er, I mean, felt sorry for me."

"So you don't really regret your actions," Sabrina accused.

"Face it, Sabrina." He licked his other paw. "This world would be a lot better off with a benevolent dictator running it."

She turned the box over in her hands as she examined it. "Dictators can be hazardous to your health, Salem. And your GPA," she added, thinking of Mr. Kraft.

*Zzzzing!* A third drawer in the box popped out.

"Wow," Salem said, cocking his head and pricking up his ears. "How did you do that?"

"I don't know." She reached into the drawer and pulled out a third note. She unfolded it and read, *"State your puzzlement aloud."*

"A puzzlement? What puzzlement?" Salem asked. "Is this some kind of party game? I'm a killer at Clue. Nine times out of ten, the candlestick is involved. And Colonel Mustard? Hardly ever the murderer." He nodded at her. "Trust me. I know these things."

Sabrina shook her head. "I don't think this has anything to do with Clue," she said. "But on the other hand, these could *be* clues. But to what, I have no idea. A little while ago, I cast a spell about finding something to help me with my school project, and this box appeared."

"Well, speaking of games, I've been out of the magic game for a while, so I can't help you." Salem yawned. "And now I think it must be time for another nap." He immediately started snoring.

Just then, Hilda and Zelda came downstairs. Their faces were covered with lavender goo, and their hair was up in curlers. They had on fuzzy pastel bathrobes and matching slippers, and they were laughing.

"Hey," Sabrina said. "I thought you two were still arguing. It's raining like crazy outside."

Zelda gave a wave of her hand. "Oh, that's natural rain, Sabrina. You know what the weather's like in Massachusetts." She smiled. "Hilda and I decided to have a little bonding experience. You know, give ourselves facials and talk about old boyfriends."

"Zelda's up to Robin Hood," Hilda informed their niece. "But I always thought the Sheriff of Nottingham was the way to go."

"Hilda, he was evil," Zelda reproved.

"But he was lots more fun," Hilda retorted. "Nobody knew how to throw a better archery tournament than the sheriff. And besides, I was never convinced that Robin was really stealing from the rich and giving to the poor." She winked at Sabrina. "I think he just made that up to attract gullible girls."

"What!" Zelda cried. "Are you implying that I'm gullible?"

As she spoke, a bolt of lightning struck the earth within inches of the Spellman home.

"Hey—hey," Sabrina said. "Would you two calm down? You're going to set the house on fire."

She picked up the box. "Do either of you know what this is?"

"Oh, my. It's our Starlight Starbright Puzzle Box." Hilda smiled at Zelda. "We won this at the Other Realm county fair oh, about two hundred years ago or so. I forgot we had it."

Zelda nodded wistfully. Then her smile faded as she pointed to the drawers. "You've started working it!"

"Uh-oh," Hilda said.

Sabrina made a face. "And you say, 'uh-oh' because—?"

Zelda moved around the couch and took the sparkling, glowing box from Sabrina. "Well, do you see this warning label on the bottom?" She turned it over and showed it to Sabrina.

" 'For Expert Witches Only,' " Sabrina read. "Oh. I mean, uh-oh." She frowned. "I cast a spell down in the basement for something to help me with my science project. How come this appeared if I'm not supposed to use it?"

Hilda moved her shoulders. "Beats me. But I'd like to get that sucker open. I left a really stunning diamond necklace in there, and I'd love to get it back."

"Let me see, Sabrina," Zelda said, thinking. "Didn't you ask us when you came home if you could cast a spell to make your teammates work together better?"

Sabrina nodded. "Yes."

"And Hilly, you want your diamond necklace back."

"Yes." Hilda nodded.

"Well, then." Zelda gestured to the box. "By working together, we can solve both your puzzles. It will be an exercise in teamwork. And we can also teach our niece another very important lesson."

Hilda frowned. "Which is?"

"A good witch—and a good leader—should be observant." She tapped the label on the bottom. "Did you read the *entire* warning?"

"Well, I would say yes, but obviously, this is a trick question," Sabrina replied. She glanced back down at the label.

" 'Warning: Starlight Starbright Is a Rainy Day Puzzle.' "

She looked up at her aunts. "I don't know what a rainy day puzzle is."

Suddenly Salem lifted his head, stretched, and yawned. "It means that if you use it on a rainy day, you have to complete it before it stops raining, or you'll be stuck wherever it sends you to solve the puzzle."

"Wherever it sends you?" Sabrina echoed.

"Yes, dear. The puzzle is a sort of problem-solving tool for magic users. When you work the puzzle, it sends you to a time and place where you can solve your problem. It only works on rainy days."

"Uh-huh," Hilda added. "And if it stops raining before you get back, you can't get back. They're very dangerous. However, they work great." She smiled.

"Oh." Sabrina quickly put the puzzle box down.

"So let's go fishing, can we, can we? Puhlese?" Salem begged. "I have the problem of not having enough fish. And I really wouldn't mind getting stuck wherever fish are."

"Too much of a good thing is still too much," Hilda said. "I almost spent the rest of my life shopping in a jewelry store, and I could see I was going to get tired of it." She rubbed her hands. "But at least I still have my diamond necklace."

"Oh, I remember," Zelda said, nodding. "We were trying to figure out if we should invest in the first shopping mall in history."

"We went for it." Hilda grinned. "It was a great invest-ment."

"Only because you kept buying everything in all the shops," Zelda retorted.

"Hey." Hilda smoothed her sweater. "We had some great deals in those stores. That's how I got my diamond necklace." She turned to Sabrina. "And you never saw better butter churns than in our mall."

"Which is why we still have three dozen of them down in the basement," Zelda replied.

"You see, Sabrina, you have to put something into the puzzle box to return both it and yourself to your starting point. So I dropped the necklace in. I forgot to get it back out," Hilda explained.

Zelda turned to Sabrina. "What problem would you like to solve, dear?"

Sabrina cocked her head. "Well, I want to get a decent grade on our project."

Zelda beamed at her. "What an admirable goal. It's so nice to see you taking after me."

"Um, and the good grade is mainly so . . . I mean *also* so I can go to Harvey's party," she added guiltily.

Hilda raised her chin. "It's so nice to see you taking after *me*."

"She'd do better concentrating on her studies than passing the centuries in endless frivolity," Zelda said.

"Oh, so she can be a stuffy egghead?" Hilda zinged back. "Life is a banquet and most people are starving."

Another bolt of lighting jagged down from the sky and set a tree on fire, just outside the door.

"Hey!" Sabrina cried. "Will you two quit it?"

"You're right, Sabrina." Zelda cleared her throat and took a deep breath. "We're not being very good role models, I'm afraid." She pointed at the puzzle box. "Let's get back to the subject at hand. Have you noticed anything about the way the puzzle box is constructed?"

"Well, it's really pretty, and the shining stars and moons are cool." Sabrina admired the box. "The hottest thing *I've* ever won at the Other Realm county fair was a cheap little plastic bottle of pixie dust."

Hilda shrugged. "Well, the fair has gotten so commercial. It's almost worse than Halloween."

Zelda nodded in agreement. "Anyway," she continued, "the little notes need to be read in a certain order. There are four of them."

"I've found three." Sabrina showed her the silvery notes.

Zelda flipped through them. "Yes, you're missing one." She reached out and tapped a fourth star.

A fourth drawer opened.

Sabrina fished out the note and read, *"Solve it and come back again."*

"There you have it," Zelda said. She took the four notes, rearranged them, and handed them in a stack to Sabrina. "Try it now."

> *As the rain falls from the cloud,*
> *state your puzzlement aloud.*
> *Solve it and come back again,*
> *before the ceasing of the rain.*

"Cool," said Sabrina.

Just then the doorbell rang. Zelda looked at Hilda and

said, "Oh, my. We're a sight. Sabrina, give us a minute to run upstairs before you answer the door."

"Okay."

Sabrina put the puzzle box down on the coffee table and walked slowly to the front door. Her aunts trotted up the stairs and disappeared around the corner.

"Hi, Sabrina," Harvey said. He was holding a dripping umbrella, and his plaid shirt and jeans were bone dry.

"Hey." She smiled. "Come on in."

Harvey stepped into the house with his umbrella. Libby swept in next, dry as toast in her cheerleading outfit, followed by Valerie, who was completely soaked. Her dark green sweater hung on her like a wet cat, and her black skirt clung to her legs. She carried their equally drenched report notebook against her chest.

"Hi, guys," Sabrina said. "Gee, Valerie, what happened?"

Valerie narrowed her eyes at Libby. "I guess there was only room for two people under Harvey's huge and enormous umbrella, which he so generously offered to share with both of us girls."

"Oh, my," Libby murmured, cupping the side of her face in a pose of dismay. "I'm so sorry, Valerie. I didn't realize you were getting a little damp."

"Yeah, too bad," Harvey said. "I had another umbrella I could have lent you."

Sabrina and Valerie traded looks. Sabrina said, "Did you get much of a *Tale of Two Cities* read?"

"Enough to know that I'm going to flunk the test," Valerie said unhappily.

"Well, maybe you'll have some more time after our meeting," Sabrina suggested. Valerie nodded glumly.

Sabrina took the umbrella from Harvey and said, "Let me put this in the kitchen. I don't want it to drip on my aunts' hardwood floors."

Salem hopped off the sofa and followed her. Once they were out of earshot, he said, "Are you going to make them something to eat?"

"Gee, I guess." Sabrina considered. "Let me see. Shall it be cupcakes or cheese doodles?"

"How about salmon puffs? Or caviar with anchovies?" Salem asked hopefully.

Sabrina chuckled. "Aren't you watching your weight?"

"Let's just say I blink at it occasionally, and leave it at that," Salem replied. "I'm sure your guests would like sushi," he added.

"Right." Sabrina pointed at the kitchen counter. Instantly a plate of chocolate-chip cookies and four mugs of hot chocolate appeared.

"Oh, sigh," Salem muttered.

Sabrina grinned and pointed a couple of cookies and a little bowl of milk in his direction.

"Don't blame me next time you weigh yourself," she warned him. Then she pointed the plate of cookies and the mugs into the air while she conjured up a tray.

Meanwhile, in the living room, Harvey said, "Wow. Isn't this a cool jewelry box?"

He picked up the elaborately decorated box that had been sitting on the Spellmans' coffee table.

"How do you know it's a jewelry box?" Valerie asked. "It looks like one of those Chinese puzzle boxes to me." She set down the wet report and snaked off her dripping cardigan sweater.

"I know because it's got jewelry in it." Harvey reached into the top and pulled out a long, golden necklace from which two or three dozen crystals dangled. He showed it to the girls. "This is really pretty."

Libby shrugged. "It's probably cubic zirconia," she sniffed.

"I don't know, Libby," Harvey said, inspecting the necklace.

When he realized she and Valerie were waiting for him to continue, he laughed and added, "I mean, I really don't know if it is or not."

"Look. These are pretty, too," Valerie said, picking up four small pieces of metallic paper. "It's some kind of poem."

She read:

*As the rain falls from the cloud,*
*state your puzzlement aloud.*
*Before the ceasing of the rain,*
*solve it and come back again.*

"Who'd like some hot chocolate?" Sabrina called, as she sailed into the room from the kitchen. "And I have chocolate-chip cookies."

"Neat," Harvey said, taking a handful of cookies. "We'll need some brain power to solve our problem."

"All we have to do to pass is get the part with the

27

Montgolfier brothers correct," Valerie said. "They really began the conquest of space."

The ornate box began to glow. "Wow. Look at that. Sabrina, what's up with your jewelry box?"

"Oh, um, it's got a special mechanism," she said biting her lower lip.

The box rose from the coffee table and hovered in the air.

"And it's weightless, too?" Valerie asked in a small, scared voice.

"Magnets," Sabrina explained. Harvey thought she sounded a little freaked out.

"Did I break it?" he asked.

"Um." Sabrina reached for the box. Harvey got to it first. His fingers pressed against something warm and he jerked, startled.

The box flew open in all directions. An eerie, blue light swirled out of it, accompanied by a strange, bell-like clanging.

"Whoah!" Harvey said. "Sabrina, what's going on?"

The blue light became a wind that whirled around the room, catching up small objects: the cookies, some potted plants, the latest *TV Guide,* and their project notebook. The things were hurled around the room as the wind dervished like a tornado.

Then, as the four looked on in amazement, the notebook landed on top of the flattened box. Valerie shouted, "I'll get it!"

She leaped forward to get the notebook, lost her balance, and flattened her hands on top of it.

And she disappeared!

"Valerie!" Harvey shouted, reaching forward.

And *he* disappeared!

"What's going on?" Libby cried.

And *she* disappeared!

"Kids? What's happening?" Hilda called from the stairway. Zelda, her face freshly scrubbed, trotted down the stairs.

Sabrina looked up at her aunts.

"Help!" she shouted.

Then she was swept forward toward the box as if by unseen hands.

And, like her friends, she vanished from sight.

Zelda glanced at Hilda. "We'd better hope it keeps raining," she said, "or we may never see our niece again."

"Will it help if we fight?" Hilda asked. "It'll keep the rain coming."

Zelda said, "I guess we should."

"Egghead."

"Airhead."

Salem sauntered from the kitchen. "What happened?" he asked.

"Sabrina and her friends got sucked into another time and place," Zelda said unhappily.

"Oh." Salem stretched and yawned as if this sort of thing happened every day. "Did they leave the cookies?"

☆

# Chapter 3

☆

The blue glow surrounded Valerie, Sabrina, Libby, and Harvey for a few seconds. They plummeted and began to free-fall in a stomach-clenching descent. Gradually their fall slowed, and suddenly they were flying and cartwheeling through some sort of tunnel or tube. Multicolored lights and images flickered through the tunnel, wrapping around the curved sides like movies projected on a screen: the space shuttle, a space capsule, an Air Force jet, a commercial airliner.

As they tumbled, Harvey shouted, "Does anybody know what's going on?"

"It, well, I'm pretty sure it's, ah, just a portal," Sabrina shouted back. "Probably a portal to er, another time and place. I'm sure it's all right."

*"All right?"* Libby cried. "Are you insane in addition to being a freak?"

*No, I'm a witch,* Sabrina wanted to say. But she

didn't dare. One of the biggest magical no-no's was to tell a mortal you were a witch, especially if you were living in the Mortal Realm. There were a few special times when it was allowed, but this was not one of those times.

*So the jig may be up,* Sabrina thought. *I may have to tell them I'm a witch if I have to get us out of this with magic. Boy, will I be in trouble with the Witches' Council. I'll be stripped of my powers and probably grounded for life. I may even get turned into a . . . newt or something!*

The pictures continued to flare and flicker along the sides of the tunnel as Sabrina flew along with the others. There was a short-haired woman with a leather pilot's cap, followed by two men in vests and flat caps who were standing beside an old-time, two-tiered flying machine.

"We're seeing images from the history of flight," Sabrina cried excitedly. "Look! That's Amelia Earhart! And those are the Wright brothers! We're going backward through the conquest of space!"

"Have you done this kind of thing before?" Valerie asked, as she hurtled alongside Sabrina. "You seem awfully okay with it."

Sabrina struggled for a reasonable answer. "Maybe I dreamed I did, so it seems familiar?"

*"What?"* Libby shouted again. "You really *are* insane!"

Sabrina made an apologetic face as they passed an image of a man in a sort of wooden hang glider.

"I know what's going on," Harvey said, grinning. "It's

a virtual reality game, isn't it? Wow, Sabrina, did your Aunt Zelda invent it?"

*Oh, thank you, thank you, Harvey, for coming up with that.*

"Okay, okay, you're onto me," Sabrina said, grinning back. "She asked me to help test it. Isn't it realistic?"

Suddenly a fresh burst of blue light swirled all around her and the others. A loud rushing like a jet engine buffeted her ears.

As Libby and Valerie cried out, they tumbled down from a brilliant blue sky about five feet above a sprawling field of tall, ripe corn.

*Whump!* They landed. One, two, three, four—Sabrina, Harvey, Libby, and Valerie—in a muddy ditch along the perimeter of the field.

"Okay, I've had enough. This is more realistic than any game ever should be," Libby said. She tried to stand up, but fell forward, up to her elbows in mud. "Yuck!"

Valerie's large, expressive eyes darted left, then right, then straight ahead. She was clutching the project report against her chest. She murmured, "I'm fainting now."

She started to fall backward, but Sabrina cupped her right hand with her left and pointed a soft, invisible cushion that prevented Valerie from getting any muddier.

Libby tried to wipe the grime off her cheerleading skirt. "This is real mud! I don't believe for one minute that I'm having a virtual-game experience!"

"You don't?" Sabrina asked nervously.

"I don't, either, Sabrina," Harvey said. "I've changed my mind." He reached for her hand. "Don't be alarmed, but I'm fairly certain we've been abducted by space aliens."

Libby shrieked and mucked around in the mud some more as she stared skyward. "Peace, space brothers!" she cried. "We're a friendly species." She scratched the tip of her nose, leaving a dab of mud on it. "Well, unless provoked."

"Or not," Sabrina murmured. Then she spied the magic box lying a distance away. It had closed back up. "Look," she said.

"That's probably their transmitter," Harvey said knowledgeably. "The thing they abducted us with."

The corn husks in the field rustled.

"And here they come," Libby said, gulping.

Sabrina got her pointer finger ready in case she had to make some magic. *As if I haven't done enough already,* she thought glumly.

Harvey pushed both girls behind himself. Then he raised one hand like Mr. Spock on *Star Trek* and said, "We come in peace."

"Don't raise your hand like that!" Libby hissed. "They'll think you're going to shoot at them."

"But he's unarmed," Sabrina pointed out.

"They won't know that." Libby's gaze was glued on the field. "They might think his hand is a laser gun."

"Well, actually, most of the aliens I've met—I mean, that I've seen described in books about this kind of thing—are very friendly." She didn't suppose she should mention that she'd been skiing on Mars a number of times. Sabrina smoothed back her hair. "Of course, I've never actually seen one in real life. Ha. Ha."

Neither Harvey nor Libby was listening to her. They were both staring at the rustling corn stalks.

The stalks began to part. Then Libby cried, "Eeek!" She grabbed onto Harvey's arm and pointed. "Look!"

Sabrina looked, and burst into laughter.

It had short horns and a square, blunt face. Its eyes were quite large. It had four legs.

It was a cow.

It stared at them without making a sound. Libby harrumphed as Harvey laughed, too.

The cow sauntered toward Valerie, who had just started to wake up. It had a long rope around its neck, which dangled and tickled her on the cheek as the cow blinked down at her.

"Moooo."

Valerie opened her eyes, saw the cow, and gave a little shriek. The cow mooed again.

She scrambled out of the way, falling off the invisible pillow and into the mud.

*Whoops.*

"What's going on?" she cried.

One eye on the cow, Libby was backing away from the cornfield as fast as she could. "We're being invaded by cows!"

"It's just one cow." Harvey walked over to it and gave it a soft pat on the back. "And look. It's friendly."

The cow looked up at Harvey and said, "Moo."

The corn stalks started rustling again.

"*Now* it'll be the aliens," Libby said. "Now that they've lured us into a false sense of security."

"*I'm* not feeling very secure," Valerie announced, also

34

staring at the cornfield. Her clothes were a mess and there was a piece of corn stalk in her hair. "Sabrina, where are we? Did I have, like, a really bad fall?"

"You could say that." Her arm at her side, Sabrina got her finger ready, just in case something dangerous came in from out of the corn.

*"Alors!"* cried a male voice. *"Où est la vache?"*

A young man strode from between the stalks of corn and stopped dead when he saw Sabrina and the others. He wore a black three-cornered hat sporting a feather over long, brown hair pulled back and tied with a black ribbon. Over a white ruffled shirt he wore a sort of black draped jacket; his black, baggy pants ended at the knee and were tied with black ribbons. He had on white stockings and leather boots.

He stared at their clothes and frowned. *"Ah, bon?"* he said in a challenging voice. *"Et vous êtes?"*

"We come in peace for all mankind," Harvey said. "We're on a peaceful mission . . . well, we don't know what the mission is . . . but we mean no harm."

"He's speaking French." Sabrina smiled. *Piece of cake. I'm taking French in school. "Bonjour."*

"Wow, he's cute," Valerie piped, smiling at him. *"Bonjour."*

Libby cleared her throat. "Cute or not—which, okay, he is—I want to know what he is doing here, and why is he dressed like someone who should be giving guided tours of Old Sturbridge Village?"

Sabrina tried to frame the question, excluding the part about Old Sturbridge Village, since she was fairly certain he wouldn't know it was a re-creation of a colonial settlement in Massachusetts.

After a few seconds of drawing a blank, she realized her French wasn't good enough. She pointed at herself and murmured,

> *"Hey, hey, what do you say,*
> *Today I can parlez great français!"*

To the young man she said, in perfect French, "We've traveled from a long way away. We're a little lost. Can you tell us where we are?"

He frowned at her. "Your accent . . . you're not French, are you?"

"Well, no," she admitted. *I guess I should have added something about an accent. Oh, well, next time.*

Then she thought to ask, "So—we're in France?"

The young man blinked. He took off his hat. "I beg your pardon?"

She frowned, a little confused. "So we're not?"

The cow mooed. "Ah, there she is," he said, walking over to her. "I've been looking everywhere for her."

"What are you guys talking about?" Harvey asked. He smiled and stuck out his hand. *"Bonjour.* I'm Harvey."

The Frenchman looked at Sabrina. "His name is Harvey," she translated. "And I'm—"

"André!" another voice shouted from the cornfield. "Where are you?"

"I'm here, master," the young man—André—called.

Two middle-aged men, in white wigs and clothing

somewhat grander but similar to André's, pushed their way through the tall stalks. *Someone is not going to be very happy about all this trampled corn.*

"What are you doing? Where is the Duchess? How could you let her escape?" the older of the two men demanded of André. Beneath a black cloak, he wore a ruby-red jacket.

"Oh, wow," Sabrina said quietly. "These guys must be French Revolutionaries. Like in *A Tale of Two Cities*, Valerie." She turned to Valerie, Harvey, and Libby. "They're trying to capture a duchess."

"Duchess!" André said to the cow. "You were very naughty to run off."

"Oh, the cow is the duchess," she explained to the others. "So it's not like *A Tale of Two Cities*."

"I'm taking notes," Valerie said. "No cow in the book. Which, frankly, amazes me. That novel's got everything else in it."

The older man turned from André to Sabrina. He glowered at her. "You are speaking English," he said to her in French. "You must be spies!"

"Uh-oh," Sabrina said to the others. "He thinks we're spies."

"Well, that's better than telling him we fell from the sky," Valerie drawled.

The man jerked his head toward Valerie. With all the jerking from one person to another, he reminded Sabrina a little of a chicken.

"What is zat you say?" he said, this time in English. "That you 'ave drop from ze sky?"

"Whoops." Valerie grimaced. "Um, not really. It's just

a little joke. Ha ha ha." She laughed weakly and looked at the others for assistance.

"Ha," Libby said anxiously, her fake smile about to crack her face in half.

"Ho ho ho," Harvey added, sounding rather Santa Clausian.

"We didn't really fall from the sky." Sabrina also smiled and, to add a little variety, wrinkled her nose.

"Then where did you come from and how did you get in our cornfield?" demanded the man, sticking with French.

"We fell off a corn wagon?" Sabrina ventured. "A hay wagon? A station wagon?" *Think, Sabrina.* "I'm sorry." She shrugged. "I can't remember how to say it in French."

"How convenient," the man replied, narrowing his eyes. "Your French has been perfect up until now. Except for your accent."

"It is quite terrible," the other well-dressed man said, making a little face. His jacket was blue. "Really, if we're going to be spied upon, it should be by people who have better accents."

"And wearing clothing which is not so strange. After all, we are French, and there are standards of style and taste to be maintained."

"I'll be sure to tell Double-Oh-Seven," Sabrina quipped, then realized she had said a very bad thing, because the three Frenchmen looked very startled.

André said to her, in a hushed voice, "You *are* a spy."

"No, it was a joke! You know—Double-Oh-Seven— James Bond." She surveyed their old-fashioned outfits

"But unless it's Halloween, or you've just been in a parade, I'm guessing you have never heard of James Bond."

"What are you saying to them?" Libby asked. "They're looking kind of mean."

"Mean?" echoed the man in the blue jacket. "We are not mean! It is simply that we 'ave worked too 'ard to allow English spies to steal—"

"Ssh," the older one said. He cleared his throat and said to Sabrina in French, "You four must accompany us to our home."

"Now what are they saying?" Valerie asked. "Because you're looking kind of freaked out, Sabrina. And I . . ." She sneezed. "I'm still in these wet clothes and you know, it's kind of cold out here." She looked around. "Wherever we are."

Sabrina thought a moment. *If we go with them, maybe Valerie can get warm, and they'll give us something to eat. And we can find out where we are.*

*And when we are. And then I can try to figure out how to get us out of here.*

She said, "They want us to go with them."

"To the mother ship?" Valerie asked anxiously.

"I don't think they have a mother ship," Sabrina replied. "But I'm willing to bet they have a fireplace."

"And maybe something hot to drink?" Valerie sneezed again.

"*Alors,*" Andre said, "the little brunette, she is sick." He looked kindly at Sabrina's best buddy. "I will give her my jacket."

He took it off and walked to her. Holding it out, he said, "*S'il vous plaît, mademoiselle.*"

Duchess the cow perked up at the sight of the jacket and nudged André's shoulder. When he ignored her, she nudged harder and he lost his footing. He tumbled forward, holding the coat above his head so it couldn't get muddy as he fell on his knees in the mud.

He laughed and nodded as Valerie stepped forward and took the jacket. "Gee, thanks," she said. "Wow, Sabrina, he's like some kind of romance hero. I feel like Drew Barrymore in *Ever After.*"

"I guess he didn't notice that I'm cold, too," Libby said, sounding miffed as she crossed her arms across her chest.

André glanced at Sabrina and gave her a lopsided grin. "That one, in the colorful court jester's clothing, she thinks she really is a duchess, eh?" he asked in French.

"She'd like to be," Sabrina replied.

"I understand." He nodded and his grin grew. "I have a sister who is very much like that."

"André, don't be friendly with the prisoners," ordered the man in the ruby-red jacket.

*"Oui, monsieur."* Andre shrugged at Sabrina, as if to say, *Whatcha gonna do?*

"I'm not so sure we can be your prisoners," Sabrina said carefully. "Seeing as how you aren't police officers or army guys or anything."

The man scowled at her. "I have no idea what a 'police officer' or an 'army guy' is, *mademoiselle,* but since you're trespassing on our land, I have every right to take you prisoner. This is the eighteenth century, after all, and the common man has rights. We are not helpless victims of fate."

"No, we are scientists!" the other wigged man announced, flinging wide his arms. "And today, we had such a success."

The other man gave him a look and cleared his throat. He looked skyward. "It's going to rain. Brother, you and I will pack up our . . . experiment. André will escort *the prisoners* home."

*"Oui, monsieur,"* Andre said, with a little bow.

The man wagged his finger at André. "And keep better watch on them than you did the cow. Duchess nearly consumed the basket."

Wearily, André replied, *"Oui monsieur."*

The two men in the wigs walked back into the cornfield. They were muttering between themselves about "security" and "Double-Oh-Seven." Sabrina didn't have the slightest idea what was going on.

André collected the cow, leading her by the rope around her muzzle, and said to Sabrina, "Please, *mademoiselle*. I don't know where you came from, or why you are here, but now you and your companions must come home with Duchess and me."

"Do I get to make a phone call?" she joked nervously.

He shrugged his shoulders. "I'm sorry, but I don't understand."

"That's all right." She started to walk beside him. "I'm sure we'll get all this straightened out," she said to the others. "As they say in all those war movies, 'Fall in.' "

Harvey smiled and saluted. "Yes, Commander Spellman."

André looked relieved as the others began to walk behind him and Sabrina.

"How far are we going?" she asked.

"Only about ten kilometers," Andre told her.

"What? That's almost five miles!" She pulled her foot out of a soggy indentation and grimaced at the coat of mud that reached up to her ankle.

"You speak an interesting dialect of French. Phone call. Fall in. Movies. Miles. We'll be there very soon," he told her.

The cow mooed.

Valerie sneezed.

Libby muttered—and Harvey walked along, smiling pleasantly.

There was a crack of lightning and a rumble of thunder. It began to rain. Hard. Libby and Valerie both moaned.

"Oh, good. The corn needed more water," André said. "I love country life, don't you?"

"Oh, yeah, bunches," Sabrina said, with a trace of sarcasm, as she watched the mud swirl around her shoes.

André looked pleased. "Then perhaps you will like to stay here, after you are released from jail for spying?"

"What's he saying?" Harvey asked Sabrina. "That those other guys are going to pick us up in a minivan?"

"He wants to know if we take sugar or honey in our

tea," she fibbed. No sense upsetting them. She'd use her magic to zap them out of here right now!

Hiding her finger, she murmured in English:

*No more wandering, no wish to roam,
here and now, let's go home!*

She wondered if they would be surrounded by blue light and whisked through the portal again. Curious, she prepared herself for liftoff, taking a deep breath of happy anticipation.

Nothing happened.

"Hmm," she muttered. She tried the spell again.

Still nothing.

"Oh, my gosh," she cried. "We left the puzzle box back in the field." *I probably need it to re-create the portal.*

"I'll go get it." Harvey turned around and loped back through the heavy rain toward the field.

André frowned. "Where is he going?"

"We dropped our . . . possession," she said. "He's going to retrieve it."

André's frown grew. "It's not a gun, is it? Or your spying equipment?"

"No, no. It's a . . . jewelry box." *Hey, maybe I can bribe him with Aunt Hilda's necklace,* she thought excitedly. *With those beautiful diamonds, he could buy a Ferrari. That is, once Ferraris are invented.*

After a minute or so Harvey trotted back.

"Sabrina," he said, panting a little and wiping his sopping hair off his forehead. "It's gone!"

*"What?"* Her stomach did a little flip.

Harvey held out his hands. "I looked all over the place."

Sabrina stopped walking. "André," she said. "That box is very important to us. May we go back and look for it?"

He looked unsure. She said, "Please?"

"Very well. I will help you."

"We'll never find anything in this rain," Libby groused.

Nevertheless, they all returned to the field and searched for the box.

But it was nowhere to be found.

*Does that mean we're stuck here forever?*

# Chapter 4

☆

☆

Back in Westbridge, Hilda and Zelda were arguing in the living room again. The puzzle box had returned without Sabrina and her friends and the aunts weren't sure what to do about it.

But each was certain that the other one's opinion about it was the wrong one.

"I think we should tell the Witches' Council what's going on and ask for help," Zelda insisted. "I'm sure this kind of thing has happened before, and they can tell us what to do."

"And I say we try to solve this on our own. We already have a less than sterling reputation as Sabrina's guardians," Hilda reminded her. "One of these days, they're going to tell us we're underqualified for the job and fire us."

Zelda looked impatient. "They can't fire us. We're her blood relatives."

"Believe me, they can fire you," Salem said as he wandered into the room. "My Uncle Louie? He got fired from being my uncle and now he's a bitter, old, lonely warlock in Wichita Falls, Texas. Used to cruise the Atlantic Ocean every season on the *QE2*. Quite the dude with the ladies. Now he just whittles on the front porch and plays the harmonica."

"That's so sad. Salem, you should visit him sometime," Zelda said.

"I have." Salem stretched and batted lackadaisically at a small rubber squeaky mouse underneath Hilda's chair. "He just ignores me. Tells me having me as a houseguest is no longer in his job description. Makes me sleep in a dog bed. He eats nothing but rattlesnake stew and watches all the TV shows I hate."

Salem gave the mouse another bat. "Plus, he's a loser."

"Salem, you should show more respect," Zelda reproved. "After all, he is . . . or was . . . your uncle."

He shrugged. "Well, he just put in an application to become a grandfather. If they can find him some kid who loves *Boy Meets World,* I'm sure they'll be very happy together."

"Hey, that's a great show," Hilda said. "I never miss it."

Salem shook his head. "Too much Corey, Corey, Corey. Not enough Topanga."

"Well, there's no accounting for taste," Hilda said. "By the way, Zelly, did my intensely trashy and poorly written Hollywood novels from Witchazon.com show up yet?"

"Yes, and they're going to make great compost after you're finished with them," Zelda replied.

Hilda smiled brightly. "I know. I love multipurpose literature." Her smile faded as she looked out the window. "It looks like it might stop raining. We have to have another argument or look up some rainmaking spells. If it stops before Sabrina gets back. . . ." She made a face. "I don't even want to think about it."

"Me neither," Zelda said anxiously.

"You could put in an application for a new niece," Salem said, then covered his mouth with his paw. "What a terrible joke. I didn't mean it." He sighed. "We have to get Sabrina and her buddies home."

Zelda picked up the puzzle box. It twinkled and gleamed, casting rainbows on the walls. "Do you suppose if we want to solve the puzzle of how to get her back, the box will send us to her?"

"It's worth a try," Hilda replied. She crossed over to her sister. She was about to tap one of the stars when she said, "Wait a minute. If we leave, and it stops raining, we'll be stuck, too. And we won't be able to help her at all."

"True." Zelda considered. "Here, we can do everything in our power to keep the rain coming down."

"You can fight like cats and dogs to make it rain cats and dogs," Salem observed.

"Isn't that strange, how both metaphors mention house pets," Hilda said.

Zelda flashed her a little smile. "Actually, Hilda, one is a simile and one is a metaphor."

"I'm sure you're wrong," Hilda insisted, almost laughing. "Well, actually, I'm not sure you're wrong. But it was a little rude of you to point out that I'm wrong."

"I just wanted to help you keep from making the same mistake in the future," Zelda retorted, chuckling.

Hilda rolled her eyes and she guffawed. "Oh, horrors, the earth would stop rotating if *that* happened."

"Ladies, ladies," Salem cut in.

"What?" they both demanded, turning to glare at him.

Lightning crashed outside and the rain came down harder.

"I'm not sure it's genuine arguing if you enjoy it," he said.

"Salem, everyone enjoys arguing. That's why people do it."

"Oh, *yeah?*" he countered.

"Yeah!" Hilda and Zelda chorused.

All three of them burst into merry laughter.

"Well, so's your old man!" Salem bellowed.

"Your mother has whiskers!" Hilda flung at him.

They kept arguing vigorously for at least an hour. But as they began to tire, Salem tapped his paw in thought as he studied the puzzle box from his place on the carpet.

*How are we going to get Sabrina home?*

After walking for what seemed like hours in the pouring rain, Sabrina and the others came upon a large stone building with a gray slate roof. Steam or smoke was rising from a large chimney on the top. There was a strange, almost sweet smell in the thick, moist air. It reminded Sabrina of the thick white paste she used to use on construction paper back in elementary school.

André said, "We make paper." He cocked his head and narrowed his eyes at her with suspicion. "But you probably know that."

"We're not English spies," she assured him. "Really and truly."

He looked doubtful. "Then why don't you have a better accent? Our competitors always send us spies with shaky accents."

"Gee, *merci beaucoup.*"

He looked apologetic. "We French, we're rather blunt, I'm afraid."

His comment surprised her. "And I thought you were just into perfume and cutting-edge fashion."

He looked perplexed. And rather charmed. "You're a very unusual person, if I may say so, *mademoiselle.*"

"Hey," Harvey piped up. "Is he flirting with you?"

"While we're all standing around in the freezing, pouring rain?" Libby added, sounding very irritated and rather jealous.

"Actually, he's telling me I have a bad accent," Sabrina said.

"Well, I can't believe you're having trouble in French class." Valerie sounded very disheartened. "I mean, if you can carry on a nonstop conversation and still be worried about the midterm, I have absolutely no hope of passing."

"You, you, you, it's always about you, Valerie," Libby said. *"I'm* freezing out here!"

"Well, look on the bright side," Harvey told Valerie. "If we stay here long enough, you'll be speaking French like a native."

At that, Valerie burst into tears. "I don't want to stay here."

She caught her breath and held out her hands, as if to steady herself. "Okay, I've been trying to be broad-minded and everything, but this makes absolutely no sense. One minute we're in your living room, Sabrina, and the next we're in what we think is France—but may be Quebec, you know. Or maybe even Haiti. And everyone's running around in pirate hats with cows!"

Duchess mooed as if she knew she was being spoken about.

Libby also started to cry.

André looked at Sabrina and said, "What is wrong with them?"

"They're frightened and they're cold," Sabrina informed him gently.

"I am so sorry. No need to be frightened. Well, yes, perhaps there is one, if you are proven to be spies. But as for being cold, I shall get you indoors immediately."

He made a sweeping bow. *"Mademoiselle,* please enter our humble paper-making factory."

"On your mark, get set, go!" Sabrina yelled, and raced for a large wooden door. She pulled it open and raced inside.

The others raced in after her. André brought up the rear, slamming the door shut against the rain as the others stopped in awe.

They were in an enormous, cavernous warehouse type of place, darkened from the storm outside. On the opposite side of the room a waterwheel was turning, and men stood at square wooden tray-like contraptions somehow connected to the wheel. Along another wall, a long stone sink was filled with rags. Men dressed in black and white, with large leather aprons over their clothes, leaned over the large wooden vats and stirred the bubbling mixture inside.

"Is this how you make paper?" Sabrina said. The scene reminded her of a witchumentary she had seen about making your own bubble bath at home. It had been hosted by Samantha Stewart—who *said* she wasn't riding on the coattails, so to speak, of a more famous relative—

"We buy rags, which we cook to a pulp," he explained. "Let me show you."

He gestured for everyone to follow him. As they walked past the row of vats, the men who were stirring nodded and greeted Andre.

Valerie sneezed and said, "I hope you two are talking about hot chocolate."

Harvey added, "Did he leave that poor cow out in the rain?"

"Wasn't that an old sixties song?" Libby asked. "Eew. It smells so weird in here. What are they doing, embalming mummies?"

"They're making paper," Sabrina said.

"At least it's warm." Valerie's teeth were chattering. "Duchess is probably freezing."

Sabrina turned to André. "My friends and I are worried about the cow."

He smiled as brilliantly as the sun. "Ah. You must be Americans!"

"Excuse me?" Sabrina blurted.

"*Oui!* Everyone knows Americans are the most tenderhearted people on earth. No one in Europe would worry so about a cow." He shrugged. "*Bon*, except for someone who was very neurotic." He laughed. "Americans we excuse for their sentimental natures."

"Really. Then you know we're not British spies?"

He nodded vigorously.

"Whoo hoo!" Sabrina cried. "Hey, guys, we're—"

André folded his arms over his chest. "I know you're American spies, and Americans are far more interested in our secret. Therefore, you are twice as dangerous."

"Your secret . . ." She glanced at the vats. "If it's something to do with paper-making, I promise you, we don't know anything about it. So even if we saw your secret in plain view, we would have no idea what we were looking at."

"Oh, now you're trying to play games," he accused.

"Harvey, Libby, Valerie," Sabrina said. "What do you know about making paper?"

The three looked at each other, then at her. "Why?" Valerie wailed. "Is there going to be a quiz? Do we get thrown in jail if we flunk it?"

"They're going to make us work here, aren't they," Libby said querulously. "Until we die of old age," Libby said, "or at least until my French manicure chips."

"Well, I hope I have to stir one of those big pots, then," Harvey said. "At least I can keep in shape until we can get back home." He looked concerned. "I just hope I don't miss next Friday's game."

"What are your colleagues saying?" André asked.

"Well, Libby and Valerie"—Sabrina pointed at

them—"are very upset and Harvey is trying to find the vat half-full."

At that moment, the door opened again, and the two older men walked into the factory. They took off their soggy three-cornered hats and thick, woolen cloaks. Two servant girls in what looked like Renaissance Fair costumes and wooden shoes clattered over and took the large bundles of wet clothing.

As the men crossed the main floor of the factory, the workers straightened and said, *"Bonjour, messieurs."*

*"Bonjour,"* the younger one said agreeably, while the other nodded absently to them as he walked over to Sabrina.

"We shall now begin the interrogation," he said.

She swallowed. "Paper is made from rags."

He blinked. "I beg your pardon?"

She moved her shoulders. "I'm sorry. I'm just nervous." Licking her lips, she said in what she hoped was an unconcerned, pleasant tone of voice, "What would you like to know?"

While she waited, one of the servant girls clattered over with a large black cane topped with an ornate brass handle and a steaming mug of something that smelled of cinnamon. Valerie groaned softly.

The man took a sip. He placed the brass tip of the walking stick on the floor and extended his left arm at an angle, striking a grand pose.

"To begin with, I want your name."

*Fair enough.* "Sa—achoo!" she sneezed, "Sabri—achoo!—na Spellman," she replied, stifling another sneeze.

The man looked shocked. He blinked at her and took another sip from his mug.

"Is this your idea of a joke?" he thundered at her in French.

"What did you say to him?" Libby demanded in an accusatory voice. "Hey, mister, we're American citizens and we have rights. We want to speak to an attorney."

"Or an ambassador," Valerie said.

"Good one, Valerie." Harvey smiled warmly. "Tell him, Sabrina. We want to talk to our ambassador."

"Zaat would be Monsieur Franklin," the man told Harvey, in English. "In Paris."

"Franklin. That sounds familiar." Valerie thought hard. Then her eyes got as huge as the bubbling vats of rags. "Wait a minute. Benjamin Franklin?"

*"Exactement,"* the man said, looking a little irritated. "Who else?"

"What year is this?" Valerie asked.

"She is 1783. What crazy question is zat?" He looked at Sabrina and said, "I think I shall speak French after all. I'm not certain I understand English as well as I assumed. Did that brunette truly ask me what year this is?"

*This isn't going very well.* "You know how it is," Sabrina said. "Time just flies when you're busy. Sometimes it's hard to keep track of the years."

"Time *flies?"* he repeated.

The other man joined them. "Joseph," he said, "what have you discovered?"

"That they are indeed spies." The man rapped on the floor with his cane. "And we must lock them up immediately."

"Hey, I don't get how you got that," Sabrina protested. "We aren't spies and you haven't proved anything."

André came up. The man named Joseph said sharply, "Yes?"

"Master, they're soaked right through and the ladies are catching cold," he said humbly. "May I take them to the kitchen for some soup?"

The two men looked at each other. Joseph turned to Sabrina. "Do I have your word that you four are the entire team here in Annonay?"

*Annonay. So that's where we are. Never heard of it.*

She nodded vigorously. "Yes, you absolutely do." *Which is very true: we're our entire science-project group.*

"It's very cold today," André pressed.

Joseph shook his head. "You are so tenderhearted, André. One might mistake you for an American."

André flashed a little grin at Sabrina, who merely shook her head wearily. "We're getting soup," she said to the others.

"Oh, yum," Valerie said happily.

"I hope it's not canned." Libby caught up her hair and bunched it into a ponytail, squeezing the water from it. "I hate canned soup."

"I sincerely doubt it will be," Sabrina drawled.

The four followed André as he led them through the factory. Beyond the bubbling vats were large groups of men pressing a white pasty substance into wooden frames lined with wire mesh.

"This is the next step in making paper," André explained. "We press the pulp into the frames and allow it to dry. We squeeze the water out much as your friend the court jester squeezed it from her hair. Then we add different kinds of coatings. We make very fine paper." He looked quite proud.

"As you may have guessed," he continued, "I am the apprentice of the Montgolfiers."

Sabrina stopped dead in her tracks. "The . . . who?"

"The Montgolfier family. They are famed for their paper." He looked hard at her. "But of course, you know everything about them. Everything *else*."

Speechless, Sabrina followed André toward a darker corner of the factory. Her heart was pounding. *These guys are the Montgolfiers, the inventors of the hot-air balloon! And this is the part of our report Mr. Kraft told us we have to get right. The puzzle box sent us here so we could get the facts right!*

She couldn't wait to tell the others. At least part of the mystery was solved.

*Will they be amazed!*

She blinked. *Wait. I can't tell the others. Because the puzzle box is a magical device—and I'm not supposed to let mortals know there is such a thing as magic.*

On their right, they passed a large area that reached to the rafters. It was roped off and draped with black curtains, and a hand-lettered sign that read, "Accès Interdit."

They all glanced curiously at it. André said, "No, no, no," in a singsong voice. Which of course made them all the more curious.

They had to go outside again to reach the kitchen, which was located in a separate building. Sabrina thought it must be terribly inconvenient—to cook all your food in one place and then have to carry it through the courtyard, in all kinds of weather, to wherever it was that the household dined.

She heard the rush of water beneath the clatter of the raindrops and said, "What's that?"

"The river, of course," André replied. He gave her a nice smile. He really was pretty cute. "You don't have to pretend to be so ignorant, you know," he said. "I know you know everything about the project."

"How do you know that?" Sabrina asked him.

"Well, of course, there's the Double-Oh-Seven part, and then you knew the code word."

*I did?*

They reached a long stone building. André climbed three steps and opened the door, went inside, and bowed chivalrously to invite Sabrina to come inside.

She entered. The room was alive with delicious smells of cooking food and a wood fire. Her stomach growled, and she pointed to it to magically silence it.

The others came in. Lavender, yellow, and soft green herbs were drying in bunches hung from a long wooden pole, and scores of beautiful pots hanging from hooks inserted into the stonework. On the far side of the room, a fire blazed. An elderly lady with a sharp profile, wearing a large white cap and an apron trimmed in navy blue over a dark blue dress, bent over a large pot suspended from a hook above the fire. She was busily engaged in stirring the contents.

"Don't let it be rags," Valerie prayed aloud.

"Or something disgusting," Libby added.

"I'm so hungry, I'd eat just about anything," Harvey put in. "Well, except maybe for rags."

*"Tante* Louise," André said to the lady. "These are some . . . visitors. My masters wish them to have something hot to eat."

*"Oui,* Monsieur André," the woman replied. She smiled pleasantly at the travelers. "I'm making mushroom soup."

"It's mushroom soup," Sabrina told the others.

"Thank goodness," Libby murmured.

"Is she your aunt?" Sabrina asked André in a soft voice.

"Oh, no." He lowered his voice to a whisper. "We just call her Aunt Louise, because she's very nice and very old."

The woman glanced at Sabrina, her face waxy-white and untanned.

*She must spend a lot of time indoors, cooking.*

She blinked, smiling, and studied the other three "visitors." Then she said to André in French, "Why are they so terribly dressed?"

"They're Americans," Andre repeated, as if that explained everything.

*"Ah bon,"* the old woman said. "I see it in the cut of the fabric." She frowned. "And what strange fabric." She slid her glance toward Libby. "That one. Is she a performer of some sort? Perhaps a lady on the flying trapeze?"

Sabrina masked her laughter with a cough. Meanwhile, Libby stood in silence, completely ignorant of the speculation about her cheerleading outfit. *Funny. Back home, her uniform is a symbol of distinction. Here, everyone thinks it looks strange.*

The cook gestured for the group to approach. In French she said, "I have a hearty soup and good, thick bread. Also, I'll make you some tea."

André laughed. "Tante Louise loves tea, just like an Englishwoman. We French, we prefer hot chocolate. Or coffee."

"Oh." Sabrina wondered if it would be rude to ask for hot chocolate instead of tea. But by then, the woman had filled a kettle with water from a wooden bucket and hung it on a hook over the fire.

"*Tante* Louise, I'll be right back," André said. "Please, watch them carefully. They're, ah, new to France, and if they left the estate they would be lost in the storm. So we want to make sure they stay with us."

"But of course." She made a little curtsy as André left the room. He opened the door and went back outside.

As soon as the door was shut, *Tante* Louise said to Sabrina, in perfect English, "Thank goodness you've come. Lord Sneakevil told me you Wouldn't be here until next week. But that may be too late. They're preparing for launch."

She grabbed Sabrina's arm and said urgently to the group, "We must do everything in our power to stop the Montgolfier brothers from conquering space!"

☆

# Chapter 5

☆

Sabrina, Libby, Valerie, and Harvey gaped at the cook. Sabrina said slowly, "My guess is your real name is not *Tante* Louise."

"It most certainly is not." The woman sniffed through her nose as if she were smelling something quite unpleasant. "I am Lady Lucretia Wormwood-upon-Rottenhamshire."

"You *are* a British spy!" Valerie cried.

The woman looked even more disdainful. "If you please, I prefer the term, 'loyal subject of the British crown.' "

"Well, that sounds like a very wordy version of spy to me," Libby said. "I don't care what you want to call it."

The woman frowned. "Why do I have the feeling you are not the crack team of professional thieves Lord Sneakevil was supposed to send me?"

60

"It's probably our accents," Harvey said. "So far, we haven't had the right kind once yet."

Her mouth dropped open. "You're Americans."

"Yes." Harvey smiled at her.

"My family lost our colonial lands in the recent war," she sniffed. "You can be grateful that peace has been declared, or I would shoot you on the spot."

Harvey looked shocked. "Wow. Harsh."

"There was a war?" Valerie asked.

Lady Lucretia looked at her. "Indeed. Have you been in a convent?"

Valerie shrugged. "A public high school. It pretty much amounts to the same thing. At least for me."

Sabrina, who had been quiet up til now, raised her hand. "Excuse me, but what did you mean about stopping the Montgolfier brothers from conquering space?"

"Nothing," she said. "I meant nothing by it."

"But—"

"And you would do well to drop the subject," Lady Lucretia said, narrowing her eyes.

"Yes'm," Sabrina replied.

Harvey pointed to the fragrant, bubbling pot. "While we're discussing this, do you mind if we eat?"

"There are bowls in that pantry," Lady Lucretia said, pointing to two narrow wooden-slatted doors to the right of the fireplace. She reached for a small ceramic bowl on the fireplace mantel and added what looked to be spices to the soup.

"I trust you don't expect me to wait on you, now that you know who I am." She sighed. "I've worked disguised as a servant for these people for two entire months. I have no idea how real servants manage it for their entire lives."

"Well, that's certainly something to think about," Sabrina pointed out. "I'm sure your own servants would like to have some credit for all their hard work."

The British woman sniffed. "Real servants are used to it. Endless hours of drudgery for extremely low pay is their lot in life, and it's what they're happy with."

"I quite agree," Libby said enthusiastically. She sighed. "It's so hard to find good help these days. Especially at extremely low pay."

"My mom says that's what teenagers are for," Valerie said.

"Not *this* teenager," Libby retorted.

"Humph." Sabrina gave Libby a look and said to Valerie, "Let's get some bowls for the soup."

The two opened the wooden doors to the pantry. There were several stacks of wooden dishes, then heaps of china, and a few miscellaneous vases and brightly painted serving dishes.

Valerie hesitated. "Which ones should we use?"

"Let's use the china," Libby said, standing behind them. "I don't eat off the cheap stuff. I'm not a servant and I'm certainly not a spy."

"I'm not so sure it's a good thing to remind Lady Lucretia of that," Sabrina murmured to Libby and Valerie both. "We're the only ones who know who she really is."

"Oh, she Wouldn't do anything to us. She's so . . . upper-class," Libby retorted, as if she knew all about situations like the one they were currently in.

"What are you three girls conspiring about?" the British woman asked sharply.

"Nothing, nothing." Sabrina grabbed up four wooden bowls. Valerie selected four wooden spoons and trailed after Sabrina.

Sabrina carried the bowls over to the pot of soup.

"Here, I'll help you." Harvey picked up the large wooden spoon in the pot. "It smells good," he told Lady Lucretia.

"You have nice manners, for an American colonist." She relaxed a little. Harvey often had that effect on people. It was one of the things Sabrina really liked about him. "I've met your ambassador, Benjamin Franklin," the woman continued. "Splendid gentleman."

Anxiously, Sabrina bit her lower lip as she stirred the soup with a long wooden spoon. Bits of tasty-looking mushrooms swirled in a thick stew.

"He's not mixed up in this, is he?" Sabrina had had a couple of adventures with old Ben Franklin, and she'd hate to think he was doing anything wrong.

"Oh, indeed not." Lady Lucretia looked wistful. "We certainly could use someone as clever as he to help us, though." She gestured to the pot. "Please, take as much as you wish."

"Thanks." Harvey smiled at her. "You're very nice, for a spy."

She inclined her head. "We simply cannot let the French lay claim to such an important invention as the balloon. They might be able to use it as a weapon against us."

"Are you at war?" Sabrina asked. *I've really got to pay better attention in history.*

"Not currently." She moved her shoulders. "However, given the temperament of the French, I have no doubt we shall be sooner or later." She raised her chin and looked steely-eyed at Sabrina. "Besides, it would damage British pride."

"Can't have that," Sabrina said to Harvey as he ladled soup into the first bowl. "Damaged British pride."

"We rule the world," Lady Lucretia said. "From sea to shining sea."

Sabrina handed the bowl to Valerie, who looked a little frightened at the immediate scowl that appeared on Libby's face.

"Here, you go first," Valerie offered, practically shoving the bowl into Libby's hands.

"Thank you," Libby said, as if of course she should eat first. She dipped her spoon into the bowl and tasted the soup. "Oh, this is just delicious. You certainly can cook, for someone who ordinarily never steps foot in a kitchen." She batted her lashes. "Just like me."

"Are you sure you aren't a duchess back in America?" Lady Lucretia asked Libby, obviously warming to her. "You certainly have the airs of an aristocrat."

"Which, to you, is not a bad thing," Libby said knowledgeably. She gave the others a snooty look.

"It's not a bad thing at all at home, in London, where people are civilized," Lady Lucretia answered. She leaned toward Libby. "But one thing I shall tell you—these French peasants don't know their place. I truly believe they're on the verge of a revolt."

"Yes!" Valerie cried, accepting a second bowl of soup from Sabrina, and keeping it this time. "It's called the

French Revolution, and . . ." Her eyes widened. "I mean, I'll bet they call it the French Revolution," she added. "If they have it. Um, maybe in 1789 or so. But I'm just guessing."

She made an "erk" face and said to Sabrina, "I got that far in *A Tale of Two Cities*." Picking up a spoon, she said, "I'll eat now."

There were some chairs scattered around the slate-floored room, and Harvey pulled them up to the fire. Wearily, the four sat and sipped their soup. Lady Lucretia produced a loaf of feather-light French bread and some cheese. Sabrina couldn't believe how hungry she was.

As they ate, their clothes began to dry. Sabrina hurried the process along with a little magic.

> *Not too fast, so they won't know,*
> *Dryer and warmer our clothes will grow.*

"Wow, I'm really sleepy all of a sudden," Harvey said.

"Me, too." Valerie's eyes half closed.

Libby yawned. Her bowl slipped from her hands and crashed to the floor.

"What's going on . . . ?" Sabrina muttered.

The room blurred. The faces of her friends grew indistinct and fuzzy, and as Sabrina yawn, the room began to dim.

*It's the cozy room and the nice, warm soup,* she thought.

Lady Lucretia leaned into Sabrina's disoriented frame of vision and said, "I'm so sorry, my dear. You seem like nice young people. But this is war."

\* \* \*

65

"You know, in all those time-travel shows on TV this stuff is easy," Hilda said, pursing her lips.

"That's because TV is fantasy, Hilda. This is reality," Zelda replied patiently.

They were in the kitchen. They had put on their witchy outfits of sparkling black and were standing over a Number 10 cauldron. The liquid inside was a rich, beautiful gold: golden memories of precious times spent together with Sabrina.

Zelda had located a very old spell in a dusty book in a crate in the basement, but some of the words of the incantation were missing. They had done their best to piece something together, but they had no idea if it was going to work.

Salem sat on the counter, his head cocked. *I didn't vote for this plan,* he thought anxiously. *If something bad happens to the puzzle box, we may never see Sabrina again!*

Hilda and Zelda had finally contacted the Witches' Council. It turned out the Starlight Starbright Puzzle Boxes had been recalled because of incidents identical to the one they were dealing with. Somehow, through an oversight, Hilda and Zelda had not received the recall notice.

Because of that, the Council had sanctioned their use of the spell in the book, even though it was incomplete and the two aunts were going to have to make part of it up. That was generally not acceptable witchcraft practice. Who knew what might happen?

Also at the Council's request, the Spellmans had magically moved their house to the top of one of the many thunderheads dumping rain all over Massachusetts. It was a safety precaution: if something went wrong, there was less chance that any mortals would get hurt.

"All right. Are we ready?" Zelda asked Hilda.

Hilda nodded and took a deep breath. Zelda held the puzzle box in her palms and extended it over the cauldron. She began the spell.

> *Mystical forces of time and space,*
> *take this box to Sabrina's place.*
> *Let her see the box appear,*
> *and read the words we wrote to her!*

*The lack of rhyme is what bothers me most,* Salem thought, his tail flicking with worry. *All the best spells rhyme.*

The two sisters raised their hands over the cauldron. It began to bubble. The golden liquid inside turned a brilliant blue, and blue foam sizzled on the surface.

But the box remained in Zelda's grasp.

"It's not working," Hilda moaned.

"Wait," Zelda told her. "I feel something. Some kind of energy."

Then *zzzzap!* The box disappeared.

The sisters cheered.

"I *knew* this was a great idea!" Salem shouted.

The house began to plummet toward earth.

As Sabrina drooped, the room suddenly swirled with blue light. Lady Lucretia cried out, "Good heavens! What's happening?"

There was a loud crack.

The puzzle box fell from the ceiling into the room—and flew into the fireplace!

"What on earth?" Lady Lucretia said.

The puzzle box doors began to open as the wood smoldered. In the room, the blue light grew more and more intense. The wind began to blow.

"Hellllp," Sabrina slurred, reaching toward the box. "Westbridge . . . Harv . . . Val . . . Lib . . ."

As the box smoked and the fire lapped at its sides, the entire thing burst into flame.

*"Nooooo,"* Sabrina groaned, lurching forward. Her knees buckled, and she fell off her chair.

Then everything went dark.

When Sabrina awoke, she was in a nice feather bed in a room painted a cheery yellow. Sunlight was streaming through a window. Something white was flopping in her eyes; she pushed it back, then pulled it off. It was a big, floppy, white cotton nightcap. She was also wearing an enormous linen nightshirt over her stiff, dry clothes. Her head was fuzzy and she felt dizzy.

*Where am I? Did I dream it all?*

There was a knock on her door. She murmured, "C'mon," and then, *"Entrez."*

The door opened, and a girl about her age with shining black ringlets and expressive brown eyes, and dressed in an elaborate gray silk gown with a hoop skirt, made a little curtsy and walked into the room. She was carrying a silver tray with a small silver teapot, a cup, and a plate with a croissant on it.

*"Bonjour,"* she said as she carried the tray to Sabrina's bed. As she placed it over Sabrina's lap, she asked, "Did you sleep well? We had to carry all of you into your rooms last night. You were dead to the world!"

"Tante Louise is a British spy. She drugged us when we discovered her secret," Sabrina said urgently. "My puzzle box is in your fireplace. I hope."

The girl cried, "Ah ha! I told my uncles you could not be spies," the girl said. "Seraphina, this will clear you!"

"Who?"

"Seraphina. Like the project."

"The what?"

The girl looked confused. "Uncle Étienne told me you said your name was Seraphina."

Sabrina shook her head. "No. I'm Sabrina. Sabrina Spellman." The room was starting to spin. She thought to herself:

> *Now's not the time to have a tizzy,*
> *Fix it so that I'm not dizzy!*

"There, that's better," she said. "Now. Let's start over. My name is Sabrina, but why would it matter if it was Seraphina?"

The girl blinked. "You truly do not know?"

"I truly do not know," Sabrina said earnestly.

"I must go and speak to my uncles at once," the girl said, rushing for the door. "Tante Louise left an hour ago to do the marketing. She has probably left forever—with our secret!"

While the girl's back was turned, Sabrina pointed the

tray off her lap and set it gently on the floor. She jumped out of bed and said, "Please, I need to go to the kitchen to check on the puzzle box. It's extremely valuable."

*"Ah bon,"* the girl said anxiously. "I'll show you on the way. Come on!"

The two girls dashed out of the room and into a sun-splashed hallway. A servant girl in wooden shoes was sweeping an immaculate floor and looking very bored. She looked familiar, and then Sabrina realized she was one of the two girls who had helped the wigged men with their wet cloaks yesterday.

When she saw Sabrina glancing at her, she turned her back and continued to sweep.

*That seems a little odd.*

They kept going. Sabrina was barefoot, at her feet slapped on the stone floors.

They left the building and dashed across the muddy ground to the kitchen. Sabrina looked down at her feet and hesitated to go up the steps, but the other girl said, *"Alors!* Hurry!"

Sabrina followed her into the kitchen. She raced to the fireplace and peered into it.

There was nothing there but piles of ash.

"Oh, no," she wailed.

"What is wrong?"

"My puzzle box—ah—fell into the fireplace after we got drugged," Sabrina said. "I tried to retrieve it but I couldn't." She slumped. "It looks like it was destroyed."

*Does that mean we're stuck here for the rest of our lives?*

The other girl looked concerned. "Oh, I'm so sorry. What a misfortune. Was it a family heirloom?"

Sabrina nodded. "Yes, you could say that."

"Well, I must go to my uncles," the girl said.

"May I come with you?" Sabrina asked. "I'd really like to talk to them myself."

"But of course." The girl picked up her skirts as they raced back down the steps. "But we must hurry. Perhaps they can still catch Tante Louise."

Back they charged through the mud. Sabrina was splattered up to her shins—but that was the least of her problems.

They entered the paper factory, passing the curtained-off area Sabrina had noticed before. Throughout the factory, the workers were already at their places, pressing the gooey paste into the wire-mesh forms and stirring the stone sink of rags to make more paste. In addition, several elderly ladies in black dresses sat on three-legged wooden stools, each with a heap of fresh, dry rags on her lap. They were chatting in French, smiling and laughing.

"Uncle Étienne! Uncle Joseph!" the girl called. "Where are you?"

"Mimi, what's wrong? And why is that girl with you?" asked the older of the two men from yesterday. "She should be locked in her room."

"Uncle Joseph, Tante Louise drugged them! She is the spy, not Sabrina."

"Sabrina?" The man—Joseph—frowned suspiciously. "You told me yesterday that your name was Seraphina."

"Excuse me, but no, I didn't." Sabrina twisted her

hands. "I don't know why you thought that, but I really am Sabrina Spellman, and I really don't know who Seraphina is."

His frown grew. "How can this be?"

"I don't know. I really don't. But your cook is really Lady Lucretia Wormwood-upon-Rottenhamshire. She's a British spy." Sabrina took another breath and kept going. "She put something in the mushroom soup she gave us last night. And my puzzle box was in the fireplace, and now it's gone."

"Burned, alas," Mimi said sadly.

Sabrina had a thought. "Maybe she fished it out and took it with her."

The man shrugged. "Why would she bother?"

"There was a diamond necklace inside," Sabrina said. "A very valuable one."

"*Alors,* I have heard that Queen Marie Antoinette has been interested in a certain diamond necklace. Can it be that you are jewel thieves?" he asked sharply.

"No, really, we are not thieves. We're not spies." She made an apologetic grimace. "Don't you think you're a little overly suspicious of strangers?"

He put his hands on his hips. "Not as a matter of course. But when they speak of falling from the sky, and when one of them tells me her name is Seraphina . . . then I am . . . *cautious,* let us say."

Before Sabrina could say anything, he raised his hand. "*Eh bien,* you insist that you did not tell me your name was Seraphina. I will allow that. But what of the falling from the sky?"

"It was a joke," Sabrina said, sounding less than convincing even to herself. "We're Americans. You know what kidders Americans are."

He didn't so much as crack a smile. She said, "Whether or not you believe me, it's true that your cook, *Tante* Louise, is a spy. She told us. In plain English, which she speaks like a native," she added.

"And you would like nothing better than for us to run around on a wild-goose chase while you steal our secrets, eh?"

"I'll go with you to find her," Sabrina suggested. "I'm a very good finder." That was not at all true. Sabrina had lost a number of things—but she had learned the hard way that you didn't call on the services of a magical finder of lost objects to help you. Then you usually had to marry them!

"You will simply try to run away," he said.

"No," she assured him. "I won't. We won't. Really."

He thought a moment. *"Bon,"* he said. "You only will accompany my brother and me. The other three shall stay here as our guarantee that you will return."

"Agreed." *What choice do I have?*

She stuck out her hand. "You have a deal, Monsieur . . ."

He laughed. "You are a splendid actress. Of course you know that I am Joseph Montgolfier, and that my brother is Étienne."

She blinked. *Of course. The puzzle box brought us to them!*

"Ha, ha." She had no idea what to say in return. Sometimes it was harder being a witch and using magic than living a regular mortal life. They wouldn't be here if they hadn't found the puzzle box. They'd just be sitting in her living room, bickering over how to finish their group project.

*Or not,* she thought. *I probably wouldn't even be living in Westbridge.*

"Well, Sabrina Spellman," he said. "I shall call my brother. We'll get out the bloodhounds and track down our mysterious cook." He sighed. "It will be too bad if she is a spy after all. It's so difficult to find good help these days."

He turned on his heel. Mimi trotted along behind him, gesturing for Sabrina to join her.

"Étienne!" he shouted. "We have an emergency."

Sabrina touched Mimi's arm. "I should tell my friends where I am. They'll worry."

"We'll send someone," she assured Sabrina, looking around the factory. She saw someone and waved her hand. "Colette, please come here."

Wooden shoes clattered on the floor. Sabrina turned at the sound.

It was the same servant who had been sweeping outside her room.

The older woman ducked her head and murmured, "*Oui,* Mademoiselle Mimi."

"Please tell Mademoiselle Spellman's three friends that she is with my uncles and me, and shall return soon."

The woman curtsied. "*Oui,* Mademoiselle Mimi."

From under her eyebrows, Colette peered up at Sabrina. Then she scurried away.

"Who is that?" Sabrina asked.

"Oh, that's Colette. She's been with us for about a year. Now, come. We must hurry. My uncles are impatient men." She laughed. "Perhaps that is why they want to learn how to fly." She gasped and covered her mouth.

Sabrina pretended not to have heard, which was fairly easy. For suddenly the morning's serenity was broken by the baying of hounds. Lots of them.

"My uncle's stable hands will be saddling the horses," Mimi said excitedly. "Come, Mademoiselle Spellman, let's be off on our adventure!" She grinned at Sabrina. "I have not had so much excitement in all my life."

"Well, I guess there's a silver lining to every cloud," Sabrina said. *And speaking of clouds, is it still raining back home?*

*I need some answers.*

*And I need them now.*

# Chapter 6

☆

As their house hurtled toward earth, Zelda, Hilda, and Salem scrambled around madly, trying to concoct an antigravity potion on the Labtop in Zelda's office before it was too late. It was very difficult to move through the rooms of the lovely old Victorian house as it wobbled and spun out of control.

"Why'd I ever bother to vacuum today?" Hilda wailed, as she clung to the edge of the desk on which the Labtop stood. The floor was like a tide of debris washed up from a sunken treasure ship—vases, rugs, jewelry, shoes, dishes, clothes, and a lot of very upset stuffed animals.

Zelda stood next to her, wearing safety goggles and straining to measure the correct amount of pixie dust into a beaker.

"Grab the canned Happy Thoughts, Hilda. I don't think we're going to be able to create any of our own."

"Speaking of vacuum," Salem said, as he crawled along the floor wearing a miniature parachute pack, "I'm thinking maybe we should abandon ship. Or house, as it were. We can ride the vacuum cleaner right on out of here." That was the standard form of transportation for twentieth-century witches, as opposed to broomsticks.

"Shame on you, Salem!" Zelda scolded. "We can't fly away from this. What if our house fell on someone?"

"If it was the Wicked Witch of the East, we'd be doing other someones a favor," Salem said. "At the very least, any Munchkins living nearby."

"He has a point," Hilda said reluctantly. "About abandoning ship, I mean. It's not looking good, Zelly. Maybe we could cast a spell to make sure the house splashes into the ocean."

"No." Zelda shook her blond hair vigorously. "I won't give up yet." She held out the beaker. "Pass the Happy Thoughts, please."

Hilda picked up a shoebox-sized box decorated with happy faces. "I hope these are still good. We haven't had to use processed Happy Thoughts in a long time. Ever since Sabrina came to live with us. With her around, we haven't needed to," she added wistfully.

She opened the box. "Oh, look, here are my sunflower shoesies." She held them up. They were sandals decorated at the toes with huge sunflowers. "Remember when we went to the day spa in the Other Realm? These are the shoesies I wore."

Zelda smiled. "That was fun. Even the part where we bickered over our facial appointments."

Hilda smiled back.

Zelda held out the beaker and grabbed the glistening memory as it shimmered in the air.

"Caught it," she announced. "Our own homemade Happy Thought."

"Wow, I'm impressed," Salem said. "We're screaming toward certain destruction and you two have a Kodak moment."

"I guess we purged all our fighting impulses with our quarrel earlier today." Hilda frowned. "But we'd better be ready to start bickering if it stops raining naturally."

"I hope the puzzle box made it back to Sabrina."

The house started falling faster.

"We'd better stop trying to be happy," Hilda said. "We're not very good at it today."

"I'll give you both an A for effort." Salem was sincere. "But would you be very offended if I jumped out of the house now?"

"Yes," they both chorused. Then they both laughed.

"Geronimo, Salem," Zelda said. "With our blessings."

Just then, a sweater of Sabrina's with his name—or, rather, claw marks—on it sailed past like a kite.

"I'm going to miss all her worldly possessions, if the house crashes," he said.

"She'll get more," Zelda said firmly.

"Absolutely. When she gets back, we're going shopping!" Hilda cried.

The air glistened. Zelda held out the beaker.

"Another Happy Thought!"

"They could have used you two on the *Titanic*," Salem said. "You would have been terrific for morale."

"Why thank you, Salem," Zelda told him. "What a lovely thing to say."

He inclined his head. "Near-death experiences make me sentimental that way."

He made his way against the whirlwind of objects, hopped up onto a windowsill, and ejected.

Joseph and Étienne Montgolfier, accompanied by their niece, Mimi, and Sabrina, spent hours riding all over the French countryside. The landscape was stunningly beautiful. The fields were ripe with crops awaiting harvest, and grapes grew on vines that would soon be plucked clean. The grapes would be made into different types of wine.

Their horses' hooves clopping on the cobbled streets, they scoured the beautiful medieval town of Annonay. They searched high and low for Lady Lucretia, but no one had seen her.

Sabrina's snow-white horse was very entertaining. She cast an "animals can talk" spell on him and they had a very nice conversation to while away the time.

His name was Antoine, and when they were far enough away from the others so that his speaking would not be overheard, he told her all the local gossip. It seemed that the mare on the farm that abutted the Montgolfiers' land was in love with Antoine's brother, Maurice. Maurice was the black stallion Étienne Montgolfier was riding.

"But Morrie is in love with Mathilde. I don't suppose you met her. She's a mule."

"Really!" Sabrina said, laughing. "How can a horse fall in love with a mule?"

"Ssh, keep your voice down. He would be angry with me if he knew I had told you. He simply can't help himself. He says it is her ears. One look at those ears and he was lost."

Sabrina giggled. Just then, Maurice looked back at them and scowled. Antoine kept his eyes very wide, very innocent.

"Ssh," he pleaded with Sabrina.

She tried very hard to keep a straight face.

"Also—and this is very hush-hush—the cow, Duchess? She's in love with André. He has no idea. She has pledged all the animals to secrecy concerning the matter, but of course, since we usually cannot converse with human beings, it has not been a difficult secret to keep."

"Well, I'm thinking that if we get stuck in your time, it might not be so bad. There's quite a lot going on. This place is like a soap opera."

She thought of Salem, who dearly loved his soaps, and felt very homesick for a moment. Her throat tightened. She cleared it and said, "I mean, you're very interesting and Mimi's very sweet."

"Ah, she will one day run away, that one," Antoine said with authority. "She yearns for the big city. She thinks Paris will be the answer to all her prayers for adventure and romance."

"What's it like?" Sabrina asked. She had only been to present-day Paris. That is to say, the Paris of the future that was her present time. When she was there.

*Whew. Time travel can be so complicated.*

Antoine shook his head. "Crowded. Dirty. Smelly. I

wouldn't live in Paris for all the gold in the King's treasury. And he has a lot of it."

"Hmm. Maybe André's right about country life being the best."

"You will never convince Mademoiselle Mimi of that," Antoine said. "Myself, I think she and André would make a good couple. But neither one of them has noticed the other."

"Mmm. Well, it's always fun to indulge in matchmaking," Sabrina said.

"It's a hobby among us French," Antoine agreed. "After all, we are the world experts when it comes to romance."

"Really?" Sabrina was amused.

"*Ah, oui.* We practically invented love."

Just then, Mimi and her Uncle Joseph turned around and cantered on their horses toward Sabrina. They had just left the outskirts of Annonay and were headed toward the river, which powered the paper factory. Mimi looked tired and worried, and Joseph's face was creased with frown lines.

"We're giving up the search," Joseph said. "She's disappeared without a trace."

*Then so has the puzzle box, if she took it,* Sabrina thought unhappily. She hated to return to Harvey and the girls with such bad news.

The two Montgolfier brothers led the way back to the factory as Mimi hung back with Sabrina. Sabrina was a little sorry for Antoine, who had really enjoyed talking. The minute she realized Mimi was planning to accompany her on the ride home, she broke the spell. Now Antoine was back to whinnying and neighing like any other ordinary horse.

As they rode, Mimi sighed, "It's so boring here. All they do is work on their experiment. I want to go to Paris." She brightened. "I could help you escape to Paris. It would be so exciting!"

"I'm not so sure that's a good idea," Sabrina said, as Antoine raised his head up and down, as if in agreement. "Paris is dirty, crowded, and smelly."

"No. It is the city of dreams!" Mimi enthused. "I could become an opera dancer."

Antoine shook his head. "Oh, maybe not such a good idea?" Sabrina translated for herself.

"I know—it sounds scandalous. But it would be fun!" She dimpled. "Do you think you could formally introduce me to the young man you are not spying with? I think his name is Arvay."

"Oh. Well." Sabrina felt a little flash of jealousy. "Um, sure. I guess."

"He is very handsome, and quite friendly." She wrinkled her nose. "Although, one must admit, he is very poorly dressed."

"Yeah, well, we've been moving around a lot," Sabrina allowed. "But as you said, we're not spies. We didn't even know where we were."

"*Ooo la-la*, you don't have to convince me any longer," Mimi said. "But you may still have to convince my uncles. They are very nervous, you see. They have almost completed their project, and they are very worried someone else will steal their glory. Their hearts are not much into the making of paper."

"They're like you," Sabrina observed. "They want something more. They want adventure."

"Ah." Mimi sat up straighter. "Then they should understand why I want to go to Paris!"

She put her heels to her horse. "Let's race back to the factory!" she called gaily.

Sabrina said, "You're on!" She felt no temptation to use magic to win the race. Seeing Mimi's excitement as she left Sabrina in the dust—or rather, the mud—made losing an actual pleasure.

Sabrina flew past the two uncles, whose horses were loping along at a more sedate speed, and dashed up to the Montgolfier compound. A stable hand caught the reins of Mimi's horse, and signaled another man to fetch up Sabrina's horse. She laughed and said *"Merci!"* as he held the horse still so she could hop off.

"Thank you, Antoine," she said in English, which was the language she had spoken with him. He winked at her.

"I won!" Mimi exulted. "Oh, isn't it glorious to go really, really fast?"

*She truly craves thrills and chills,* Sabrina thought. *I wonder if there's some way I can help her—without getting either of us in big trouble?*

"I'll race you into the factory," Mimi said. "My uncles keep sweets in their desk drawers. I know all their hiding places."

"Okay." Sabrina darted after Mimi. "Oh, and by the way, do you know where my shoes are?"

"I'll give you some of mine," Mimi told her. "Annonay is famous for its leather. We have lovely shoes made for us by the dozens. I have so many shoes I can't even count them."

"Wow. This is paradise," Sabrina said.

*"Non, non.* Paris is paradise."

They raced into the factory. The elderly ladies in their black dresses smiled and greeted Mimi. So did the vat stirrers. Clearly, she was a favorite with everyone.

"My uncles' offices are this way," she told Sabrina. "Hurry, before they get back here and catch us!"

"I think I'm in enough trouble with them already," Sabrina said uncertainly.

"Oh, fooh! This is the stealing of candy, not scientific secrets."

Just as they reached the curtained-off area, Sabrina detected the familiar clatter of wooden shoes. The canvas moved strangely, and a head popped out from behind it.

It was Colette, the servant who had been sweeping in the hall and who had been trailing after them when they had left to find Lady Lucretia.

Her face reddened as she caught sight of Sabrina, and she jerked her head back behind the canvas.

"Hey," Sabrina said. Before she thought about what she was doing, she untied the curtain's edge and dashed inside.

"Oh, my," she gasped.

In front of her was the enormous, drooping shape of an unfilled hot-air balloon. It was beautifully stitched together from hundreds of panels, each secured in place with row upon row of buttons. It was dark blue, with big golden faces and suns bordering the center.

Beneath the balloon, the servant in the wooden shoes was running away from Sabrina, her arms loaded with large rolled-up documents.

"What are you doing?" Sabrina demanded.

"Mind your own business, Fräulein," the woman said over her shoulder in a thick German accent. "I was here first."

Sabrina ran after her. "Here first? What are you talking about?"

"If you want to steal the blueprints, you are too late," she said triumphantly. "I, Grete von Schnoopen, have beaten you to it!"

"Oh, no, you don't!" Sabrina shouted. She pointed at the woman, who started skidding on the floor as if it were coated with ice. Her wooden shoes could not find purchase, and she tumbled in a heap to the floor.

"No one is stealing any blueprints," said a deep voice behind Sabrina. It was Joseph Montgolfier.

*"Ach,"* the woman said in dismay, as the scrolls rolled away from her grasp . . . with a little help from one nearby half-witch.

And as they rolled, the puzzle box was revealed for all to see.

"Oh." Sabrina pointed at the floor to make it unslippery again, ran across it, and grabbed up the puzzle box. It was badly burnt, but it appeared to be all in one piece—or at least, the one piece it was when the drawers were closed.

*I hope it still works,* she told herself fervently.

"What is that?" Joseph Montgolfier asked, extending his hand. "Give it to me, please."

"Oh, no," Sabrina said in a quick breath. "Please, it's my jewelry box."

He looked dubious. "You are in the middle of the countryside with no coat, no means of transportation, but you have your jewelry box?"

"It's mine," Grete von Schnoopen said. "She tried to set it on fire, but I saved it just in time."

Joseph held the box against his chest. "Please. What kind of fool do you take me for?" he asked the German woman.

She shrugged. "Well, you *are* French."

"And you *are* trying to steal the secret of our smoke balloon," he said sarcastically. "Therefore, not someone prone to honesty."

Sabrina's brows knit. *Smoke balloon? I thought those balloons were filled with hot air.*

*No wonder we got an F on our project.*

"Hey, if she retrieved my jewelry box out of the kitchen fireplace, she's been in there recently," Sabrina said. "She may know where Lady Lucretia is, Monsieur Montgolfier."

He glared at the German spy. "Well?"

"Long gone. I helped her escape myself," she sniffed. "We were partners in this enterprise."

"And you have both failed," Joseph said, with obvious pleasure.

Grete von Schnoopen raised her chin. "Even though you have defeated me, Montgolfier, my beloved home-land will soon possess the secret of the smoke balloon, and we will fill the skies with them."

She threw back her head and cackled wildly.

"Never," Joseph said fiercely.

In his anger, his knuckles turned white as he tightly gripped the puzzle box. Sabrina swallowed and said, "Um, please, sir, may I have my jewelry box?" *Before you crush it into magical matchsticks?*

He pursed his lips. "I'll consider it."

"Uncle Joseph?" It was Mimi, who skidded to a stop in the doorway. "What is happening?"

"Go to the factory floor and find André. Tell him to get the magistrate. We have another spy in our midst."

"Colette?" Mimi asked incredulously, staring at the woman. "But you've been such a wonderful servant! She sweeps like a professional, Sabrina. You should see her."

"I learned it in spy school," the woman said proudly.

"After all, she's a von Schnoopen." Joseph glowered at her.

Mimi turned to Sabrina. "They are a famous family of spies. They have all graduated with honors from the Rhinelander Spy School. Colette, I can't believe this of you!"

The German spy raised a hand and pointed to Sabrina. "She's a spy as well. She told me so!"

"I did not," Sabrina said. She looked at Mimi. "I can see why your uncles are so paranoid, though. This place is crawling with spies. Um, don't you have background checks in this time?"

"Mimi, go," Joseph ordered.

Mimi took off. He said to Sabrina, "Here is your jewelry box, *mademoiselle*."

87

"Oh, thank you," she said gratefully. As she accepted it from him, she accidentally tapped one of the stars.

The box began to glow.

"What on earth?" Joseph blurted.

*Oh, great.*


The house was still divebombing earthward. Hilda looked out a window and said, "At least it's still raining."

"Another Happy Thought," Zelda said. But they both just smiled sadly at each other. Their potion did not appear to be working at all.

Then, suddenly, the house froze in space. Everything inside slammed around, ricocheting off the walls, smashing and crashing.

But the house hung in midair.

"Wow. Way to go, Team Spellman," Hilda said, startled. "We've saved the day."

"And the house. Maybe it was that last Happy Thought." Zelda beamed at her sister. They high-fived each other.

"We can do this," Zelda said.

The house slowly rose.

"Whoops, wrong way." Hilda looked at Zelda. "Now what?"

Just then, Salem drifted past the window in the rain, his parachute deployed. He cocked his head and said, "Hey, ladies, what's the haps?"

"We're not sure," Hilda replied. "We seem to be stuck."

"Hmm. Let me see if I can think of something." He

looked down. "As I slowly make my way through the thunderstorm."

He disappeared beneath the window.

Lightning crackled and zigzagged past the glass.

"Ouch!" Salem shouted.

Then another bolt of lightning flashed, and hit the house with a bone-shaking crash.

☆

# Chapter 7

☆

As the glow from the puzzle box illuminated the room, Joseph Montgolfier drew closer. "What is causing that?" he asked, in a curious, interested way.

*Like one scientist to another.*

Sabrina cleared her throat and gestured with her head toward Grete von Schnoopen.

"Maybe we can talk about it later," Sabrina suggested.

"Ah, of course." He looked abashed, as if in his quest for knowledge he had forgotten the presence of the enemy.

Sabrina glanced anxiously down at the glowing box.

In the ensuing silence, thunder rumbled. Joseph cocked his head, listening, and looked frustrated as another rumble passed overhead.

"Can't test the balloon again today, eh, Montgolfier?" the German lady sneered. "What a foolish place to work on your invention. It rains constantly here."

"It beats Seattle," Sabrina said. The other two looked at her with bewilderment on their faces. It occurred to Sabrina that she didn't even know if Seattle had been founded by 1783.

*I'm really going to study harder if I get home,* she promised herself.

*Not if. When.*

The sky was still threatening rain about half an hour later, when some tough-looking men showed up to escort Grete von Schnoopen away to the Annonay jail. There she would await trial for espionage. She and her guards were accompanied by a French nun in a large, starched hat that reminded Sabrina of a paper airplane.

After the little group was gone, Mimi reappeared, goggle-eyed, and complained to her uncle, "André wouldn't let me come back into the room. He said it was dangerous!"

Joseph looked pleased. "Well, the lad has a head on his shoulders after all. I'll have to reward him."

Mimi stamped her foot like a little girl. "Finally, something exciting happens around here and I miss the whole thing."

"Excitement and danger are close companions," Joseph said gently, "but not fit companions for my precious niece."

Mimi rolled her eyes. "Oh, such old-fashioned talk. Sabrina, you would think we were living in the Middle Ages."

"Well, you almost are," Sabrina observed, then caught herself. "I mean, in the middle of one of the most exciting ages to be alive."

"It's boring. Incredibly dull," Mimi insisted. She put her hands around her uncle's arm. "Come to the kitchen, Uncle Joseph. I'll make hot chocolate. Since we no longer have a cook." She shook her head. "And now, with Colette—I mean, Madame von Schnoopen—gone, we lack another servant, as well."

"As you wish, my dear." Joseph smiled adoringly at her. "Come with us, *mademoiselle,*" he invited Sabrina. "We'll examine your jewelry box by the light of the fire."

Indeed, it had grown dark in the factory, as the clouds lowered toward the horizon.

"First," Mimi said, "Sabrina must have shoes."

She ran off to fetch some. André left to accompany her, and Sabrina decided to try a little matchmaking, as she and Antoine had discussed.

"André's really intelligent," she ventured.

"Indeed. He's a good apprentice. Not too good a shepherd though," he added fondly. "We took a smaller version of the smoke balloon out for a test in that cornfield yesterday," he explained. "We had tied the lead line to Duchess. But it came loose and she wandered off. We had quite a time of it." He chuckled. Then he yawned.

"We still haven't mastered the production of the smoke," he confided. "It's so difficult to maintain a fire aboard the balloon. They keep burning up."

"Look!" Mimi cried, holding out an exquisite pair of little black-heeled shoes with gleaming silver buckles. "Are they not perfect for you?"

"They're gorgeous," Sabrina said. "But I can't put them on my dirty feet."

"There is water in the factory," Mimi said. "Come. You can wash your feet."

"I'll accompany you," André said, trailing after them. Sabrina smiled to herself, assuming that André had finally noticed Mimi, and hoping for some vice-versa.

Then, as Mimi went on ahead to get a fresh bucket of water and a clean towel, André caught up with Sabrina.

He said, "Those shoes will look magnificent on your feet, *mademoiselle*. But of course, anything you wore would be enhanced by your beauty."

Sabrina's lips parted in shock. "Excuse me?"

"I went with Mimi to make sure she chose the loveliest pair for you," he went on. His eyes shone. "She was very happy to part with them for your sake. As I would be, if I had anything that you would ever care to possess." He sighed. "Such as my heart."

"Pardon me?" she squeaked.

"I shall never leave your side," he promised. "I will become your shadow, *chère* Sabrina Spellman."

*Uh-oh.*

Mimi returned with the water. "Please," she said, drawing up a three-legged stool for Sabrina.

Sabrina sat down carefully on the stool and put the glowing puzzle box beside it.

"This feels good," Sabrina confessed, as she washed the dirt off her feet. "I'd love to take a bath."

"Oh, we'll have some servants draw one up right away," Mimi said.

"Only if it's not too much trouble," Sabrina said.

Mimi shrugged her shoulders. "The river is behind the factory. All they have to do is carry the buckets back to the house and up several flights of stairs to the bathing room."

"Oh—that's all?" Sabrina said weakly.

"Look," André said, pointing. "A little drawer has opened in your puzzle box."

"Oh." *How did that happen?* Sabrina tried to act calm. But her heart pounded as she spied a little note inside. It was written in Aunt Zelda's handwriting—and on Zelda's personalized stationery!

*I'd better read it in private,* she decided. *But I'm just itching to see what it says!*

"I'll just shut it for you," André said, shutting the drawer.

"No!" she cried, uncertain if she could get it open again.

But it was too late. The drawer was firmly closed.


Valerie paced. "I think they've sold Sabrina to the Gypsies, and we're next," she fretted.

"You really are a geek," Libby snorted. "Where do you get these crazy ideas? Selling Sabrina to the Gypsies. Hah. Besides, those two brothers seem like good businesspeople. If anybody around here should be sold to the Gypsies, it should be me."

"Well, *something's* happened to Sabrina," Harvey said. "We haven't seen her since that English spy lady fed us knockout *soupe du jour.*"

However, since then they had been treated rather well, especially for spies. Harvey had to admit that. They'd had a great breakfast of croissants and hot chocolate and an even better lunch of ham and cheese quiche, fried potatoes, and baked chicken, among other things.

But he was getting antsy just sitting around, and he was very worried about Sabrina, just as Valerie was.

"If someone doesn't take us to Sabrina soon, I'm going to look for her," he announced.

They had been sternly ordered by Étienne Montgolfier to stay in their rooms, which were in the east wing of the house. The west wing was forbidden, just like in the movie *Beauty and the Beast*. Harvey decided it might be some kind of French custom to keep the western portion of your house off-limits. It was a custom he wished they would adopt in Westbridge.

*Since my room's on the western side of our house, I'd never have to worry about cleaning it for company.*

At the moment, they had gathered in Valerie's room, after discovering that the locks on their doors were very flimsy and easily broken. As she had no chairs, they were sitting on the floor. The sky was clouding up and the distant, rolling hills rumbled with thunder. It made Harvey edgy. He got to his feet.

"Okay, that's long enough. I'm organizing a search party for Sabrina."

"I'm on it," Valerie said, jumping to her feet.

Harvey and Valerie looked at Libby. She took a deep breath and made a great show of getting to her feet.

"I suppose I'll go with you. After all, we shouldn't get separated if we can help it."

"Thanks, Libby. You're a great sport." Harvey patted her on the back.

" 'Great sport' is my middle name," she said, sounding pleased.

"Huh. I never knew that." Harvey smiled at her and Valerie. "Okay, let's go."

They opened the door and crept into the hall.

"Now what?" Libby asked.

"West wing or bust," Harvey said firmly.

Behind them a voice growled in beastly English, "You are going where?"

They jumped and turned around at the exact same time, just like the gang on *Scooby Do*. Their inquisitor was none other than Étienne Montgolfier.

"Uh-oh," Valerie breathed.

"We want to see Sabrina," Harvey said. He pointed at the man for emphasis. "Right now."

*"Bon,"* Étienne said, with a little bow of his head. "Ze *cuisine*. Ze 'ot chocolate."

"Hot chocolate?" Libby folded her arms across her chest. "She's been enjoying herself while we've been cooped up in here, worried sick about her?"

He appeared confused. "You wish ze 'ot chocolate?"

She smiled sweetly. "Do you people use the little marshmallows?"

*"Pardon?"* he said in French.

"Never mind-ay-voo," Valerie cut in, shaking her head at Libby. *"Oui, merci.* Hot chocolate."

*"Bon."* He gestured for them to follow him down the hall.

So they did.

A second bolt of lightning hit the Spellmans' Victorian as it hovered in the air. The house shook from the force of the electricity, but otherwise it was undamaged.

"Thank goodness our lightning rod worked," Zelda said, pressing a hand over her heart. She leaned out the window and spotted Salem's parachute, a small dot below her in the rain.

"Salem," she called, cupping her hands, "are you all right?"

"A little toasty," he shouted back up to her. "I think I used up one of my nine lives."

The parachute caught a current and sailed at an angle toward the ground.

*"Hasta la vista, baby!"* Salem called to the two sisters.

"Well, nothing appears to be the worse for wear," Hilda said, smoothing her sweater. "Now all we have to do is get the house down." She looked around herself at the mess. "And do some cleaning."

"I don't understand why we're having problems with gravity," Zelda mused. Then her eyes widened. "Yes, I do."

She started rummaging through all the things on the floor. "Where's that feather duster? Sabrina was using it just before her friends came over. We must have residual magic in the air, Hilda. From the puzzle box."

"Of course. Sabrina and the others were dealing with the conquest of space." Hilda joined Zelda in the search. "After it came back, we had problems with conquering space ourselves."

"That sounds reasonable." Zelda's eyes widened. "Complicated and inconvenient, but reasonable."

"Here," Hilda said brightly, then realized she was holding an old magic wand instead of the feather duster.

97

She squeezed the side measurement to see how much charge was left.

"This thing's bone dry," she commented. "We should give it to the leprechauns for their recycling program."

Zelda nodded as she dug through the mess. "Yes, that's nice, Hilda, but please help me find the feather duster. Ah ha! Here it is."

She raised it up and gave it a little wave.

The house began a very gradual and civilized descent.

"High-five, Zelly!" Hilda cried.

"High-five, Hilly!" Zelda cried in return.

"Are we bad or what?" Hilda did a little victory dance.

"Let's make sure no one can see this," Zelda added.

She moved her arms. Clouds swarmed around the house, blanketing it in a thick cocoon, as it drifted toward its foundation on the Spellmans' property.

"Well, this certainly is one for the Spellman family history book," Zelda said. She sighed. "Speaking of which, I wonder how Sabrina's doing?"

Sabrina was in the kitchen with Joseph Montgolfier, who was laughing as he tossed little scraps of paper into the fireplace. The heat of the fire made them soar and dip, much like a modern-day hot air balloon.

"So you see, the smoke lifts the balloon," he said. His face was red from the heat of the fire. He crossed to the kitchen table and picked up a little box he had deftly stitched from some taffeta, blew it open, and then dropped it over the burning logs. It, too, rose above the flames.

Idly, Sabrina folded a paper airplane and aimed it toward the fire.

"Ah, you know something of science!" he cried. "I am impressed, *mademoiselle*."

She shrugged. "Um, it's nothing."

"This is boring," Mimi complained as she stirred the hot chocolate on the stove. "Let's talk about Paris. In Paris they have dozens of stores devoted to the selling of shoes. Can you imagine that?"

The door to the kitchen opened. Étienne Montgolfier came in, followed by Harvey, Valerie, and Libby.

"Hi!" Sabrina said, running to greet them.

She gave Harvey and Valerie each a hug, but as she neared Libby, the cheerleader said, "Ew. Excuse me, but I'm here for the hot chocolate."

"We were all worried about you, Sabrina," Harvey told her.

"I wasn't," Libby insisted.

"Harvey stood up to Mr. Mountgolfball and told him he'd better take us to you or else," Valerie filled in.

"Harvey. That's so heroic," Sabrina said, giving him a little kiss.

Mimi flushed and looked away.

He beamed. "Gee, thanks. I can also break eighteenth-century bricks over my head, if that would also impress you."

"We got bored," Valerie explained.

"What have you been doing?" Harvey asked.

"Well, we went horseback-riding and then I helped catch another spy." She smiled. "And I found the puzzle box."

She pointed to it. It was sitting on the kitchen table, glowing away.

Libby made a face. "I don't know what that thing really is, but I don't care, if it can help us to get home."

"Why is it glowing?" Étienne asked, bending over the box. His brother stood beside him. "Is there a candle inside? Is it burning from within?"

"I was just about to ask *mademoiselle* for an explanation," Joseph said. "She claims it is a jewelry box."

"Yes," Sabrina said. "Really. My diamond necklace is inside."

The two men appeared completely uninterested in her mention of diamonds. Their heads were almost touching as they bent over the puzzle box. Étienne picked it up and turned it over.

"How do the stars and comets sparkle so?" he asked, examining it. "What is the mechanism?"

Sabrina moved her shoulders. "I'm sorry, but I really can't say." *Well, at least it's not a lie.*

"It's a delightful work of engineering, is it not, Joseph?"

"Indeed, Étienne. One can't help but appreciate the craftsmanship."

"They sound like those guys in the computer club who talk about how much memory they have," Sabrina said.

"Only, they also belong to the French club." Valerie sighed. "I swear, Sabrina, I don't understand a single word. Even when they say *'Oui.'* "

Sabrina wished she could let Valerie know she had cast a spell on herself to speak fluent French. *I guess that's always going to be one of the difficulties about living in the Mortal Realm. That, plus not being able to use my magic freely.*

She was itching to get her hands on the box and find out what her aunts had written her.

"And look! This little drawer has extended." Joseph put his hand inside. "There is a note." He set his jaw as he inspected it. "'If this box should go away,'" he read.

The two brothers looked at Sabrina. "What does that mean?"

She hesitated. "Kind of like, 'This jewelry box belongs to,' the way we say it in English."

"Ah." He shrugged and put the paper back in the drawer.

At that moment, André burst into the room. He said, "The repairs on the trial balloon have been completed." When he saw Sabrina, he lit up like the puzzle box. "Good evening, *chère* Sabrina. How are you?"

"Hey, what's he saying?" Harvey asked, sounding jealous.

"Tomorrow at dawn we shall have a new test," Étienne announced. "Children, you are about to witness history in the making."

*Then will we go home?*

# Chapter 8

☆

As Hilda and Zelda pointed the house back to order—repairing dishes and crystal and putting them back in the hutch, sending Sabrina's stuffed animals marching back up the stairs, and a hundred other chores—they watched the Weather Channel. Their favorite weathercaster, Jason "the Tan" Mann, was in a lather . . . over their town.

"I'm renaming Westbridge, Massachusetts, *Wet*bridge, Massachusetts," he said cheerily. "Will the rain never stop?"

"Not if we can help it," Hilda muttered. She snapped her fingers and lightning zapped into the ground outside the parlor window.

"Yow," Salem cried, stirring out of a deep sleep. "Would you two *please* stop that!"

"How long is it going to rain in Westbridge?" Jason Mann continued on the Weather Channel. "Forty days and forty nights? Ha ha!"

Hilda cocked her head. "He is *so* tan. I guess no one's warned him about skin cancer."

Salem stretched and yawned. "Sometimes warnings go unheeded. Don't smoke. Don't eat yellow snow. People warned you two about that puzzle box. Told you to throw it out, didn't they?"

The two sisters glanced at each other. "You know we didn't get the callback notice, Salem."

Salem drew himself up and looked indignant. "How soon they forget. I told you to throw it away as soon as you won it at the fair. I knew that box was going to be trouble the moment I laid eyes on it."

Hilda pondered a moment. "That's true. I remember now. You did."

"And I was right, wasn't I?"

"I think we even decided to throw it out," Hilda recalled. "We just never got around to it."

"Oh, dear." Zelda sighed. "Then it's really our fault Sabrina's in this mess. Like when you leave scissors out around a little child."

"Or chocolate-chip cookies around a dieting cat," Hilda added.

"Hey," Salem groused. "Enough with the 'fat cat' jokes, okay? They're extremely tasteless."

"Good thing, or you'd probably eat them, too," Hilda teased. Then she grew more serious. "We blew it, Zelda."

"We're going to have to make it up to her," Zelda announced.

Salem drawled, "I believe there's going to be a party at Harvey's in a couple of weeks. A big bash Sabrina very much wants to attend. However, she has been threatened with house arrest if her grades don't improve."

Hilda wrinkled her nose in a mischievous, playful way. "Parties are very important at her age." She thought a moment. "Or at *my* age, for that matter. We'll let her go no matter what her grades are—okay, Zelda?"

Zelda was horrified. "What? And teach her that there are no consequences for her actions? Forget about the scissors, Hilda. Just hand her a chain saw!"

Thunder as loud as cannon fire shook the rafters.

"Will you two please . . ." Salem began, then muttered, "No, this is a good thing."

Then, despite all the noise, he went back to sleep.

In the middle of the night, Sabrina carried a candle in a candleholder and the puzzle box into the corridor outside her room. By the light of the candle, she pressed the stars and comets, wincing as the blue light flashed up and down the hallway, half-expecting to be whisked somewhere else in time and space.

Instead, all four drawers opened, and she fished out four notes. All were written in her Aunt Zelda's handwriting.

"Okay," she murmured, and read:

> *If this box should go away,*
> *This is what you ought to say:*
> *Magic box, you must appear,*
> *In this time of now and here.*

Sabrina took the notes and put them in the pocket of her linen nightdress. "Thank you, Aunt Zelda," she whispered.

For the first time since they had landed in France, she slept well.

Above her bed, as a good witch should.

In the eighteenth-century village of Annonay, the next morning dawned bright and clear. As André hooked the hot-air balloon up to a wagon—not the cow—the Montgolfier brothers crossed their fingers for good luck.

As the sun rose and the dew glistened on the grass and lovely autumn leaves, a large crowd had gathered to watch the launch. Grouped in the morning chill just outside the paper factory, the hopeful spectators murmured in anticipation. There were laborers in loosely woven shirts, richly attired merchants, and ladies in hoopskirts and gentlemen in floppy jackets and white wigs. An old man leaned on a cane and ate a piece of fluffy white bread while a very small boy watched him with big, eager eyes.

Sabrina was nervous for the brothers. This was their first public attempt at flying the balloon. Already they were busily stuffing straw into the brazier they had built into the neck of the balloon. The smoke had nowhere to go but into the main cavity of the balloon itself, and the large, dark blue sphere was rapidly filling up.

"Now this *is* exciting!" Mimi said, slipping her arm through Harvey's. "Everyone is watching the experiment! It will be the talk of all France."

Harvey looked uncomfortable as Mimi continued to glom onto him. He said to Sabrina, in English of course, "I wonder—if this works, do we get to go back to Westbridge?"

André stood close to Sabrina and murmured, "I feel as though I am in some wonderful dream."

"André!" Étienne said sharply. "You're needed."

André whispered, "I shall return, my dear Sabrina." He walked with pride toward the balloon-launching area.

Joseph Montgolfier handed André a pitchfork. "Help pitch in more straw."

Sabrina was amazed that the balloon, which was made of linen and lined with paper, hadn't already caught fire. *I don't know what happens next,* she realized, *even though this was part of our report. Maybe we deserved that F.*

She tried to decide if it would be all right if she pointed a fire out if one occurred. On the other hand, she wasn't supposed to use her powers to help people gain riches or fame.

*But if it's a life-threatening situation, I will put it out. Even if it changes history.*

That was a scary thought. If history changed, would they be stranded here forever?

"This is so strange," Harvey continued. "Today I've decided I'm dreaming," he said. "If it's not a virtual-reality game and we haven't been abducted by aliens, there's no other answer." He went pale. "Except for a brain tumor!"

"I don't think you have a brain tumor," Sabrina assured him. "I think I'd go with the dream scenario."

"Well, except that I usually dream I'm a rock star." He shrugged sheepishly.

"Then maybe the dream's not over yet," Sabrina said.

"Look!" Valerie cried. "It's going up!"

The balloon was completely full. The crowd cheered as it began to rise. And then it went up, up, and away!

"My uncles are geniuses!" Mimi crowed, squeezing Harvey as she jumped up and down.

"Yeah, it's really neat," Harvey answered happily. He grinned at Sabrina. "Awesome. We're watching history being made."

André pushed through the crowd to return to Sabrina's side. "Is it not a miracle?" He was ecstatic.

"It's wonderful." Sabrina was sincere. The Montgolfier brothers were hugging each other with tears in their eyes. It was great to see how thrilled they were at their success.

"The conquest of the air has begun," André said. *"Vive la France! Vive Montgolfier!"*

"Long live the Montgolfiers," Sabrina returned. "Long live France."

They all watched the balloon continue its ascent. The crowd ran along its route as it drifted away from the factory. André took Sabrina's hand, and Mimi grabbed Harvey's, and the two French young people hurried the two Americans along.

"Come on, Valerie," Libby said, irritated. "I guess no one's going to hug us and tell us 'Vive la France,' but we might as well keep up."

"He gave me his jacket," Valerie muttered, as she and Libby jogged along. "I kind of thought he liked me."

"Well, I don't care if he prefers Sabrina," Libby insisted. "The last thing I need is a boyfriend who lives in eighteenth-century France."

"You have a point," Valerie said wistfully. *But she can afford to be picky. She's Libby.*

Everyone ran cheering to the cornfield. The balloon was falling very fast, casting a shadow on the ground. *If this is a dream, it's very realistic,* Valerie thought. *But how else can this be happening?*

"So, okay, they didn't go up in overstuffed chairs, and now that we know that, why are we still here?" Libby added, as the balloon whomped down on the ground and the crowd went berserk. They lifted the Montgolfier brothers on their shoulders and carried them through the field, as André took possession of the balloon by holding onto the basket. He threw back his head and laughed.

"And why do I think that question makes any sense at all?" Libby went on. "Because these kinds of things do not happen to Westbridge cheerleaders as a rule." She looked at Valerie. "Or Westbridge social outcasts, either."

"True," Valerie agreed. "But it certainly has been an interesting dream. I wonder which one of us is really having it?"

Libby frowned. "Well, I figure I am, except that usually I dream I'm very rich, very famous, and married to Ewan McGregor."

Valerie brightened. "That's amazing! I do, too."

*"Oh."* Libby made a face. "Maybe it's time for me to upgrade."

Valerie wilted a little. Then Sabrina walked over to them and said, Um, this might sound odd, but I think *I* know why we're still here."

"I haven't woken up?" Libby said.

Sabrina looked uncomfortable. "I think we have to rewrite our essay, and put it inside the puzzle box," she said. "Mr. Kraft told us we had to do it over and get our facts on the Montgolfiers correct. So we're here to get the facts, but we haven't written the essay."

"That makes as much sense as any of this does," Valerie said, shrugging. She turned to Libby. "Neither one of us is married to Ewan McGregor."

"Well, after all the excitement dies down, I think we should go back to the factory and grab some paper." Sabrina laughed a little. "There's a lot of it there. And we'll just write it all down and then—"

"Look!" Valerie shouted, pointing at the crowd. "It's Lady Lucretia Wormwood!"

Sabrina turned. A hooded figure had just turned away, and was making her way through the crowd.

"Mr. Montgolfier! And the other Mr. Montgolfier!" Sabrina cried. "André! Mimi! She's here!"

But no one was listening. Everyone was too busy celebrating. By the time Sabrina made her way through the crowd to where the figure had been, the spy was long gone.

# Chapter 9

☆

Just then, André caught up to Sabrina. His eyes were shining and his face was red. He looked about as happy as someone could be, and not float away.

*Or do only witches do that?*

"*Mademoiselle,*" André said. He flushed. "I wish to ask you a very important question."

"Okay." She waited. He remained silent.

Then he flung himself on one knee—in the mud—and clasped his hands in front of himself.

"Marry me."

Sabrina's eyes widened.

"Um, André, let's talk about this privately," she suggested.

"But we're speaking French. They don't understand a word," he said. He smiled at her. "Now that our work has succeeded, I can take a wife."

*Oh, dear.*

"André, you're really sweet," Sabrina began, "but—"

Just then, Harvey walked up. "Hey, Sabrina, Mimi keeps saying the same thing over and over. I don't understand what she wants."

Sabrina raised her brows questioningly. Mimi flushed a deep scarlet. She took Sabrina by the arm and led her a slight distance away.

"I want to marry Harvey," she said shyly. "Will you tell him? I know it's not done that way, that the man must ask, but . . ." She made a little gesture with her hands. "I am afraid he will slip through my fingers, do you understand?"

"Ah." Sabrina hesitated. "Well, here's the thing, Mimi. And André," she added, as he drew near. "See, Harvey and I are kind of . . . going steady."

Mimi frowned. "I'm sorry? You are what?"

*This is really awkward.*

"We're dating. We go out."

"You are engaged?" she asked, touching her chest and looking pale.

"No. We're too young."

Mimi blew the air out of her cheeks. "But you are certainly not too young. You're practically an old maid!"

Mimi looked over her shoulder at Harvey, who gave her a smile and waved at her. "You see? He loves me!"

Before Sabrina could stop her, she ran back over to Harvey and threw her arms around him. He looked at Sabrina in astonishment.

"Tell him!" Mimi cried.

"Tell me what?" Harvey said.

Libby and Valerie traded glances.

"I'm saying, 'Duh,' " Libby muttered. "And also 'dream on, Mimi Montgolfier.' "

Sabrina walked over to the couple as André trailed behind her.

"Sabrina, you cannot love another," he cried. "You cannot!"

"Harvey," Sabrina said levelly, "Mimi wants to marry you."

*"What?"* Harvey said, staring down at Mimi.

"Oh, I am humiliated!" Mimi cried. *Obviously, she doesn't need a translation.*

Mimi let go of Harvey, whirled on her heel, and ran.

"This is the weirdest dream I've ever had," Libby muttered.

"Gee, Sabrina, I didn't lead her on or anything," Harvey said anxiously.

Sabrina patted his arm as André caught up with them. "That's okay, Harvey. André wants to marry me, and I—"

*"What?"* Harvey said again.

"I really think it's time to get the heck out of eighteenth-century France," Sabrina muttered.

"Let's go write that essay," Valerie suggested, "if you think that will end this nightmare. Because I couldn't agree more."

Meanwhile, back in Westbridge. . . .

"Will it never stop raining?" Jason "the Tan" Mann shouted into the microphone as the cameras rolled.

He was standing in front of Westbridge High School, a brick building with a stair-step facade that resembled their old stomping grounds in medieval Amsterdam, to Zelda's way of thinking. The floodwaters had risen to a level just above the windows on the ground floor.

The fact that the school had been closed because of the floods was causing jubilation among the students. And "somehow," Valerie, Libby, and Harvey's parents were convinced that their teenagers were camped out in the Spellman house, safe and sound.

Meanwhile, water swirled and rushed down the streets of Westbridge—carrying along newspaper vending machines, trash cans, and even park benches. The rain runoff had turned into a river without end.

"Westbridge is drowning!" Jason Mann went on.

"Well, not exactly," Hilda said, with a guilty shrug. "If it were, we would stop making it rain, right, Hildy?"

Wearing yellow rain slickers, they both stood up to their knees in water in their living room. Hilda carried Salem in her arms. His fur was ruffled and he kept pleading, "Don't drop me, for the love of heaven. I hate water."

"Oh, you're such a fraidy-cat," Hilda said to him.

"Exactly. Accent on cat. Cats are not fond of water. Please remember that," he begged her.

Zelda slogged over to their sofa, thought about sitting down, and shook her head. She said reluctantly, "Do you think we should stop making it rain?"

"No," Hilda replied. Her tone was firm. "No one's been hurt, and Sabrina will be stuck if it stops."

Zelda nodded. "Agreed," she said with relief. "Well, what shall we argue about now? We've almost run out of things to disagree on and chide each other over. If nothing else, this certainly has cleared the air between us." She smiled at her sister. "I had no idea how angry I was with you for losing the pen Albert Einstein lent me."

"This makes me nostalgic for the seventies," Hilda said. "Remember all those encounter groups we used to go to, to share our pain?"

Zelda rolled her eyes. "Please. Don't remind me. The clothes we wore then. Ugh."

"You have a point." Hilda laughed. "Remember leisure suits?"

"Ghastly," Zelda said.

"Hey. I looked great in them," Salem insisted.

The sisters tittered. "You looked terrible. And those platform shoes!"

"Cutting edge," he sniffed.

"Polyester lounge lizard," Hilda hurled at him.

"Hey, it doesn't work if you argue with *me,*" he reminded her.

"True." She made a face.

"However, for the record, you both looked like shepherdesses in those flouncy ruffled blouses. They did nothing for either one of you," he said.

"Hey!" they both chorused.

*I'm still the king of the comeback,* Salem said to himself.


Meanwhile, in France . . .

Sabrina had been hunched over the essay for some time. Writing with a quill pen, it had taken her almost twenty minutes to write one page. Mr. Kraft's minimum for a passing grade was five pages—his *minimum.*

Her hand cramped up and her quill became blunt. She decided to ask Mimi if she had another.

But as she stood in the doorway of Mimi's room, she saw that the Montgolfiers' niece was crying. A large trunk was open on her bed, filled to the brim with beautiful gowns, shoes, and jewelry.

"Going somewhere?" Sabrina asked gently.

"Go away." Mimi blew her nose on a silk handkerchief. "Or have you come here to gloat?"

"Why would I do that?" Sabrina came into the room. "Mimi . . ."

"Mimi!" Étienne Montgolfier shouted, tearing into her room. "Ah, *mademoiselle*, hello. I have wonderful news. The King and Queen have summoned us to Paris. We are to perform another launch of the balloon for them at the royal palace of Versailles!"

"That's *fantastique*," Sabrina said. "Congratulations!"

"It is a triumph. We are to leave tomorrow morning." Étienne raised his brows. "But Uncle Joseph must have told you, Mimi. You're already packing."

"Paris?" she asked with shining eyes. "We're really going to Paris?"

"Really and truly," he said proudly. "Lay out your most beautiful dress, Mimi. You are going to meet Marie Antoinette and Louis XVI!"

"Wow, this is some parade, huh, Sabrina?" Harvey asked, as they sat in one of four coaches bouncing and jostling out of sight of the Montgolfier paper factory.

"Do you think we should tell Marie Antoinette to leave France?" Valerie asked nervously. "Because I got to the part in *A Tale of Two Cities* about her getting her head chopped off."

"Ew," Libby said. She touched her throat. "It's okay if I wake up now."

Just then, André clopped up on Antoine and tipped his hat at Sabrina. *"Bonjour, mon amour,"* he said sadly. Then he clopped away.

Seated at the window, as far away from Harvey as possible, Mimi made a great show of staring out the window.

"I don't think you'd better," Sabrina said to Valerie. "It might change history."

"Oh. Okay." Valerie frowned. "What are you talking about?"

"Nothing," Sabrina said. She had resumed writing the essay in the coach, using the hard surface of the puzzle box like a desk. Her hand began to cramp again, and she stopped to make a fist.

"Here, Sabrina, let me take over," Valerie suggested. "We'll each take a turn."

Grateful, Sabrina handed her the blotchy paper, a fresh quill from Mimi's supply, a bottle of ink, and the puzzle box.

"Be careful," she cautioned Valerie. "You know you get carsick if you do homework on the bus."

"Okay," Valerie said.

The trip to Paris was long and arduous. Also, extremely bumpy. It didn't take long for Valerie to call it quits. Harvey volunteered to work on the essay for a while.

Sabrina fell asleep many times. She lost track of the number of times they stopped to eat and rest.

And then, suddenly—

"Paris!" Mimi cried.

Only it was not the Paris of books and songs. Even from the outskirts of town, Paris smelled. The streets were clogged with carriages, riders on horses, and beggars. The people were thin, tired, and hopeless. The buildings were filthy.

"Oh," Mimi said, shocked. "This is not at all what I expected."

Sabrina translated what Mimi was saying to Valerie, Libby, and Harvey. Valerie replied, "It would be what she'd expected, if she'd read *A Tale of Two Cities*. Only I guess it hasn't been written yet."

Sabrina chose not to translate that in return.

And then they were in the countryside, traveling through a beautiful forest to Versailles. The enormous palace complex was absolutely stunning, with Grecian statues, wide vistas of marble, and gardens filled with fountains and canals.

"Oh, it is much lovelier here," Mimi said, sitting up straighter.

"Yes, but it's a fantasy, really," Sabrina replied. "The people live in filth and poverty, while the King and Queen live like, well, the King and Queen."

Mimi seemed pensive. "Fantasy, and reality," she said. "Some people live in dream worlds." She glanced at Harvey. "I guess that is what I have been doing. Foolish Mimi."

She looked out the window and sighed.

They finally arrived at the palace entrance, where they were greeted by a servant who showed them to their rooms.

117

"Wow," Valerie said, as they walked into enormous bedrooms decorated with scenes of Greek gods and goddesses. "This is fancier than the fanciest hotel I've ever been in."

"It *is* nice," Libby allowed, bouncing on her bed. "Hmm, if a bit bumpy."

"We shall have the exhibition in one hour," the servant informed them. Then he clicked his heels and departed.

Sabrina and the other girls refreshed themselves and dressed in some of Mimi's nicer dresses. They met Harvey and André on the way to the garden. André looked longingly at Sabrina, and Mimi sighed when she caught sight of Harvey decked out in her uncle's castoff formal attire—white wig, black jacket, black knickers, white stockings, and black heeled shoes.

Then André looked at Mimi, and she at him, and they drew closer together. Sabrina cocked her head, watching them, straining to eavesdrop.

André said to Mimi, *"Mademoiselle,* would you permit me to escort you to the launch?"

"With pleasure, *monsieur."*

They spoke rather formally to each other, but they seemed comfortable in each other's presence. As they walked away, Libby sniffed, "Where are *our* escorts?"

"Well, *I'm* here," Harvey said innocently. Sabrina hid a smile. He was such a good guy that he missed half of Libby's broad hints that he should treat her like his special girl.

Then they were at the launching area. The beautiful balloon which had been used in Annonay was replaced by one even more beautiful. But it *stank!*

Sabrina soon learned why: to make the smoke even thicker (and therefore, more "powerful") the Montgolfier brothers were burning rotten meat and leather shoes in addition to the wet straw and damp wool. The smell was terrible, and all but the most stouthearted had moved a very good distance away.

Special observation areas had been built for the exalted onlookers—dukes and duchesses, princes and upper-class commoners. An orchestra of men in white wigs played courtly music.

"The King and Queen of France!" a man in formal velvet clothing announced.

"Wow, check out her hair," Libby murmured.

Queen Marie Antoinette was wearing an enormous wig topped by a miniature hot-air balloon. Sabrina would have laughed if she didn't think doing so might get her head chopped off.

All the observers bowed. A little child tottled around, dressed in satins and lace, and everyone chuckled as its mother grabbed it up, murmuring profuse apologies to the royal couple. They smiled at her, indicating that they weren't at all put out.

"Too bad they're going to get their heads chopped off," Valerie said sadly. "I think this history project's gotten a little too up close and personal for me."

"The launch will begin shortly," Joseph Montgolfier said.

"This is cool," Harvey told the others, "even if it is just a dream. We know everything about the Montgolfiers now!"

"True," Sabrina said.

"And I'm almost finished with the essay," Harvey added.

Sabrina had a flash of insight. She said, "I think part of solving this puzzle is learning to work as a team. Why don't you let Libby finish the essay? That way, each of us will have worked on it."

"Sure, Sabrina." He smiled at Libby and gave her the paper, the puzzle box, and the other supplies.

Libby made a face and said, "I'm going to go sit in the shade. It's too sunny here."

"They're getting ready," André said to Sabrina. "We have decided to send up passengers."

"Oh, how exciting," she told him.

"*Oui.* A duck, a cockerel, and a goat." He looked proud.

"Libby, be sure to put that in," Sabrina called, as Libby made herself comfortable under some trees.

"Okay, okay," she groused.

"Sabrina, I must go and help my employers," André said. Then he paused. "You know, Mimi, she's a nice girl, and well, she's French. . . ."

Sabrina smiled at him. "I think that's a very good idea. Go for it."

He blushed a little. "You speak such odd French. But you do have style."

"Gee, coming from a Frenchman, I'd say that's quite a compliment."

"André!" Joseph Montgolfier bellowed.

"Coming!" He dashed off.

"Sabrina, what did he say to you?" Harvey asked, sounding a little jealous.

Sabrina grinned. "He's going to ask Mimi out. Or whatever it is they do to get acquainted."

Harvey shrugged. "Actually, they get married. Just like that." He snapped his fingers.

As if on cue, Libby screamed. Sabrina and Harvey whirled around.

"Help!" she shouted. "Someone stole the puzzle box!" Libby cried. She pointed into the trees.

Sabrina and Harvey ran over to her. Without hesitation, Harvey dashed into the trees while Sabrina asked a few questions.

"How did they get it away from you?"

"Just yanked. Two black-gloved hands came from between the trees."

"We have to put the essay inside the puzzle box to get home," Sabrina said.

"At least in your version of this nightmare," Libby retorted.

Harvey ducked back out. "I don't see them."

Valerie ran up. "What's going on?"

"Someone took the puzzle box," Sabrina said. "Let's spread out and search for them."

The other three nodded. "I'll go this way," Libby said, pointing to the area where the fountains were.

"I'll go back into the trees."

"I'll cover the waterfront," Valerie said. "Or rather, the path back to the palace."

"And I'll go check out the crowd," Sabrina said.

They parted ways. Sabrina was checking out all the beautifully dressed onlookers, when suddenly there was a drumroll, followed by a cheer. Sabrina spared a glance.

The balloon was going up!

It was about ten feet above the ground, when above the cheering someone started shrieking.

"My baby!"

It was the same woman whose toddler had amused the king and queen. She pointed at the balloon.

Her little child was aboard!

Without a moment's hesitation, Sabrina ran to the rope that was dangling beneath the basket, grabbed onto it, and started climbing. Then she pointed at the rope and said,

> *Right now you're slack as a black adder,*
> *Go straight and angled, like a ladder.*

As the onlookers gasped, the rope became a stairway that Sabrina climbed up. She hopped into the basket and pulled the child into her arms.

"Witch!" someone yelled. "Witch!"

The crowd took up the chant. They were fast becoming dots on the ground to her.

Angry, frightened dots.

*Uh-oh. I'd better not go back down there again. But what am I going to do?*

Then she remembered the spell her aunt had sent her with the puzzle box.

> *Magic box, you must appear,*
> *In this time of now and here.*

It worked! The puzzle box appeared at the bottom of the basket.

*Now what?*

"Sabrina!" Harvey yelled. He waved his hands on the ground. "They caught the thieves! But they don't have the box."

"I do!" She showed it to him. Then she pointed him up, up, and into the basket.

"Whoah." He looked disoriented. "I'd ask you how you did that, but since this is a dream, I'll just go with it." He smiled at the little kid, who was a girl with curly black hair. "Cute kid." Then he frowned. "It sure stinks in here. Does she need a diaper change?"

"No. It's the rotten meat the Montgolfiers decided to use for fuel."

"Yuck." Harvey shuddered. "It's really bad, Sabrina."

In short order, she pointed Valerie and Libby into the balloon. She said to Libby, "Finish the essay."

Libby pulled out her quill pen. "I have, like, two sentences left." She held her nose. "That smell is so terrible, my eyes are watering."

Meanwhile, the crowd was chanting, "Witch! Witch!"

Sabrina said to the others, "I can't go back down there. Those people know . . . I mean, think, I'm a witch."

"Can you blame them?" Libby said.

Harvey moved his shoulders. "You *have* been doing some pretty weird stuff, Sabrina."

"Well, I'm betting that if you finish that essay and we put it in the puzzle box, we'll be transported home. But what do we do with the little girl?" Sabrina asked.

Suddenly a wind whipped up. The balloon was tossed like a feather, and everyone inside screamed.

"We'd better put more hay and stuff in the burner," Harvey said. "They didn't plan for this much weight in the balloon."

He began to pitch more and more hay inside the brazier. The balloon went aloft again.

Then it burst into flame!

The crowd gasped. Sabrina was about to point it out, wondering what would happen if they fell back to earth, and trying to think up the right spell, when a familiar voice cried out, "I'll save you, Sabrina!"

It was André, in another balloon. *They must have had a backup, just in case.*

He was rising fast, and he came abreast of their balloon. "I don't have enough fuel to keep aloft with all of you aboard," he said.

"Let me give you the baby, then," Sabrina suggested.

"I'm finished!" Libby cried.

"Yes!" Sabrina dropped to the floor and worked the puzzled box. The four drawers opened, and then the top. Sabrina took the essay from Libby and dropped it inside.

*Whoosh!*

They were surrounded by blue light. Back through the tunnel they rushed, moving forward past the images of the conquest of space—the Wright brothers, Amelia Earhart, fighter jets, space shuttles—

—and then with a *crack!* they appeared over Westbridge High . . . in the burning balloon, in the middle of a fierce rainstorm.

"Wow," Valerie cried as thunder and lightning crackled around them. "We're back."

"Where are we?"

It was André. His balloon had somehow been pulled into the vortex with them. He and the little girl had been yanked into the present!

*Uh-oh,* Sabrina thought. *Now what?*

☆

# Epilogue

☆

Take a look at this!" Jason "the Tan" Mann cried into the television camera. "Two hot-air balloons, one on fire, caught in the jaws of the rainstorm!"

Hilda, who'd been watching the TV—which she had levitated—from the vantage point of their rowboat, jostled Zelda, who'd been reading, and cried, "It's Sabrina!"

"And the rain is putting out the fire as the passenger in the other balloon is coming aboard, pulling a daring switch with a blond-headed girl!"

"Who's that?" Zelda asked, as they studied a boy dressed in late-eighteenth-century clothes. "He's handing a baby to Sabrina."

They watched as the boy expertly guided the damaged balloon to the roof of the school. Then Sabrina's started to descend as well.

"Get out the vacuum," Zelda said to Hilda. "We're going over there."

By the time her aunts arrived (landing in a hidden spot), Sabrina had the situation well in hand. Mr. Kraft, who had also been watching TV at home, came barreling down to the school. On camera, he promised A's to his "intrepid science students."

He also wanted to know who the French kid was.

"André. The foreign exchange student, remember?" Sabrina said. "And his baby sister?"

Mr. Kraft looked puzzled, but since the cameras were rolling, he beamed and said, "Of course."

Hilda and Zelda rushed up to Sabrina.

"Are you all right, dear?" Zelda asked, rushing up to Sabrina as she stood under the eaves of the school with her friends.

Sabrina sighed and walked a short distance away from the others with her aunts. "The Witches' Council is really going to let me have it," she said unhappily. "I had to use magic in front of these guys and the townspeople of Annonay to—"

"Hey, Sabrina, how'd we get here?" Harvey said. "I thought we were going to work on the project at your house?"

Hilda winked at Sabrina. "Part of the spell is that mortals don't remember any of it. We'll think up a clever excuse to explain the balloon ride," she whispered. "Your friends always buy them."

"Now I know where I should have gone to be coached on showing remorse for taking over the world," Salem said.

"And it'll be nothing to send Andre and his baby sister back to their own time," Zelda added. "We've done that kind of thing before. It's just basic witchcraft."

"She's not his sister," Sabrina said, but she realized it didn't matter.

André blinked at her. In French, he asked, "Do I know you, *mademoiselle?*" He looked anxiously around. "Where is Mimi, the girl I love?"

Sabrina smiled to herself. *Well, all's well that ends well.*

Without waiting for another second to go by, she *zapped!* the puzzle box out of existence.

"I'll pull the rest of my grades the old-fashioned, mortal way," she said. "By studying."

"Then you've learned your lesson," Zelda said. She looked at Hilda. "And no matter what happens to your report card, you can go to Harvey's party, with our blessings."

"Woo hoo!" Sabrina cried. "Let the good times roll!"

*Is it great to be a witch or what?*

# About the Author

Bestselling author NANCY HOLDER has sold forty-one novels, including two other *Sabrina, the Teenage Witch* novels: *Spying Eyes* and *Scarabian Nights*. She also has Sabrina stories in *Eight Spells a Week* and *Millennium Madness*. Working solo as well as with her frequent coauthor, Christopher Golden, she has written many *Buffy the Vampire Slayer* novels and books. She has also sold over two hundred short stories, articles, and essays. Her work has been translated into over two dozen languages, and she has received four Bram Stoker awards for her supernatural fiction.

A native Californian, she lives in San Diego with her husband, Wayne, and their three-year-old daughter, Belle. In their spare time, all three Holders work out at the gym and read books—and no one ever sleeps.

*A fun-filled guide
to the mystery and
magic of the universe!*

## Sabrina's Guide
## to the Universe

Using my magic, Salem and I traveled
through outer space and now we want
to share our discoveries with you!

by
Patricia Barnes-Svarney

**From Archway Paperbacks
Published by Pocket Books**

2316

# I'm 16, I'm a witch, and I still have to go to school?

Sabrina The Teenage Witch®

## Look for a new title every month
## Based on the hit TV series

## From Archway Paperbacks
## Published by Pocket Books